The Sentinels

Radicci Sisters Mystery, Volume 12

M.E. Purfield

Published by trash books, 2024.

This is a work of fiction. Similarities to real people, places, or events are entirely coincidental.

THE SENTINELS

First edition. December 20, 2024.

Copyright © 2024 M.E. Purfield.

ISBN: 979-8224892242

Written by M.E. Purfield.

Also by M.E. Purfield

Auts Series
Auts
Books About Everyone
The Satellite
The Ableism of Salvation
What Sorrow Flies Off Roofs
The King of Dodgeball Goes with the Flow
When the Lights Go Out

Blunt Force Kharma
Bound Kharma
Kharma's Pursuit
Kharma's Glitch
Kharma's Gatto
Desolate Kharma
Blunt Force Kharma

Cities That Eat Islands

Cities That Eat Islands (Book 1)
Cities That Eat Islands (Book 2)
Cities That Eat Islands (Book 3)
Fish Hunt
Cities That Hide Bodies
Complete Cities That Eat Islands

Miki Radicci
A Black Deeper Than Death
In a Blackened Sky Where Dreams Collide
Blood Like Cherry Ice
Surly Girly
Bawling Sugar Soul
A Girl Close to Death
Heart on the Devil's Sleeve
Sinking Stones in the Sky
The Ghost and the Stream
Expressway Thru the Skull
Hacker's Moon
Miki Radicci Shorts
The Ultimate Miki Radicci Omnibus Vol 1
The Ultimate Miki Radicci Omnibus Vol 2

Miranda Crowe
Bagged

Munki Moo Moo
Munki Moo Moo

Radicci Sisters Mystery
Psychic Sisters
My Dead Body
Saints
Squeezed
Broken Psychic Hearts
The Emptiness Above
The Sludge Below
Doe
Auties
The Killer
The Deceiver
The Sentinels
Favors
Bumper
Rats In The Cage

Short Story
Natural Born Killer
Limits of Stupidity
MiLK
Orange Flecks

Through Tangled Nerves
The Creative
Defective Brain Club
Line
The Van Outside
Doorway Down
Just
Short of a Long Holiday
Lifetime Hallmark Scheme
Malignant Little Bastards
Pain Killer
Sibling Rivalry
Hole In The Head Freak
Neurodivergence on FH-358

Stories
A Sandwich Can't Stop A Bullet
The Morrows
How To Make Friends with Teenage Anarchists

Tenebrous Chronicles
Party Girl Crashes the Rapture
Angel Spits
Six Feet
Tweens with Pop Guns
Lightning From The Fire
The Subject

Tenebrous Two
Darby & Cain

The Saoirse War
Ealu
Thainig An
Ag Dul Abhaile
Buama Ama
Fealltoir
Spas Reoite

Standalone
Breaking Fellini
Delicate Cutters
Jesus Freakz + Buddha Punx
Buddha Punx + Ghetto Girlz
Klepto Pyro Mojo
The Pick-Up
(R)Evolution
Angst

Watch for more at www.patreon.com/mepurfield.

Deepest thanks to my Patreon supporters who make this story possible. Mike Mallory, Christy Lynn Margaret, Ann Purfield, and Allen Richards; you are the best!

Powder Burns

She expected this to happen. Not like this but in some way. Her job is dangerous. Life is dangerous. She did not seem to care. She always cares for others more than herself. For some reason. Maybe she has low self esteem. I understand that. I am glad she has it. If she did not have it then I would not be here now. She would not have rescued me from Elite and their special projects division. I would still be living in the dormitory. Switching from the East to the West Coast. Still having my rare psychic ability tested. Still living with no friends or family. No future.

Now I would return to all that to bring my sister back. To have her awake. Instead of lying on the hospital bed with machines monitoring her vitals and tubes nourishing her body.

I would do anything.

• • • •

I was home when I first heard about the standoff on St Pauls Avenue. Jordan found the news story on her cell phone. It popped up on her Facebook. It was a local story and all her friends were stoking it with Loves and Shares and gossip. I hate social media for lots of reasons but I give it credit for that moment. The media reported three people were possibly holding two other people hostage in a house. It was not until later when I texted Miki on the phone I knew it was her held hostage. She was on assignment for Tenebrous. An assignment that turned out to be more than she expected.

I rushed down to St Pauls. It was only a few blocks away from my house. Jordan came with me. She is such a good girlfriend. I am a lucky girl. As we ran down Baldwin Avenue she called her stepfather Raymond Resnick. He works for the FBI. He always make me nervous but not because of his badge. He knows that Jordan and I are a couple. Jordans mom has no clue about it. Everyone in my family and circle knows about Jordan and I and they accept us. They accept me and my sexual preference. But Jordans mom is in the dark. In the closet you might say. Or maybe Raymond told her. Maybe she accepts it and practices discretion. Or maybe he hides it from Jordans mom for a reason.

Anyway. Raymond knew about the stand off on St. Pauls but he did not know Miki was involved. He told Jordan he would find out what was going on and call her back. Jordan and I stood at the safety barrier. We shoved our way through the people who stared at the offending house hiding behind a wall of hedges down the block. Their stupid mouths gossiped. They probably hoped for a shoot out. They got it. Shots were fired but the bullets never reached us. The sound of guns pierced my soul. Weakened my legs. Was Miki shot. Did she shoot someone. Because of some strange side effect of her psychic ability to experience anothers pain and death she tries not to kill. The act of murder screws up her ability.

I later learned that Miki was not shot.

Maybe she should have been since the house exploded.

• • • •

THE SENTINELS

I ran through the barrier to the burning house. Jordan pulled my arm. Tried to hold me back. She wanted to keep me safe. I wanted to save my sister from the inferno.

Cops stopped us. Blocked us without touching us. Since I was born without a voice due to my autism Jordan shouted over the sirens and the screams and the oxygen hungry flames and told them who we were. My sister was in the house. The two cops believed us but told us to keep back. They brought us to a tented section where men in suits spoke to each other or on their cell phones. One of them wanted to talk to us about Miki.

Jordan watched and worried over the firemen fighting the fire. The fire brought the two other levels down on the first. The fire no one could survive.

I paced. I shook my hands and kicked my feet. I squealed and screamed. My brain spun with a billion possibilities. A billion ways that Miki could survive the explosion. My brain focused so hard the rest of the world faded into electrical static. I screamed. I pounded my head. My brain refused to reset. I needed help. I needed control. I needed my sister in my life. I dropped to my knees and tried to hit my skull on the concrete. Nothing else was harder. It should reset my brain. It should stop my meltdown.

Cops pulled my arms. Pulled me back. I shook. I jerked. I attacked. I screamed. Sensitivity ruled my brain and body. It made me a wild animal. Jordan demanded they let me go. You were not supposed to restrain an autistic when they went into a meltdown. But cops being cops ignored her. They did their job. Performed their training. Took control of the situation even if it hurt or killed someone. They saw a hysterical and violent black woman. How else were they trained to handle someone like that.

When I came to. When my surroundings returned to my brain. I lay on the sidewalk. My hands were cuffed behind my back. Jordan sat next to me. Her delicate hands were on her lap. Tears coated the cheeks of her beautiful mixed Asian face. She held up her phone. With my brain I could call into it and talk to her with a speech app. Yes. My brain is weird. That is part of my rare psychic ability. Nature replaced my ability to speak with the ability to enter cyberspace. If I was born over a hundred years ago I would be a normal autistic teen.

I shook my head. My body was exhausted. My eyes were heavy. Embarrassment soaked my heart. Everyone probably thought I was a nutzo retard. How I hoped Jordan refused to see me like that. The way she petted my head and kept my curls from my face tempted me to believe she loved me still.

Jordan called over the cops and demanded that they uncuff me. They did. And just in time.

Frantic voices from the rubble called out We got a survivor.

• • • •

Two survivors.

My sister and Mike Mallory. She and Mallory were lucky. They were found in the doorway of a secrete concrete room in the basement. Like they were hiding during an Earthquake. I had no idea who Mallory was and why he was in the house. Ruby Stahl later said that he was working with Miki. Ruby is sort of Mikis supervisor at Tenebrous. She explained the whole story. Mallory is part of her team. He was supposed to protect her and help find this girl with mad psychic ability.

THE SENTINELS

Whether he performed a good job is debatable. His efforts won him a broken leg and multiple bruises and cuts. Mostly on his head.

Miki escaped with no broken bones except for the fracture in her skull. Her brain swelled. The doctors induced a coma to help alleviate it. It worked but now she remains in a coma.

She has been in a coma for the last two months.

• • • •

Jordan and I lay on the couch in the living room of our old Victorian house. Since Raymond discovered her sexuality she insists we spend less time at hers. She is scared that her mother will walk in on us during a private moment. He had a lot of private moments there. We are into each other. We have been together for almost five months if you include that time she went away for a while. I love Jordan. I have and will do anything for her.

The television plays a Korean television show all the kids have been talking about. It is on Netflix and I am not impressed with the foreign movies and shows they have been showing. Sometimes I get lucky and they show one of my favorite Asian directors latest films. But luck runs short along with my patience for voice dubbing.

Sitting in Jordans arms and kissing her lips and tongue is a welcome distraction. I would like to do more. So would she based on the way her hands move up and down my body. But Lorelei and Darby are in the kitchen making dinner. Lorelei and Miki have been friends for years. Miki also legally arranged that if she should ever die that Lorelei becomes my guardian. If

Miki dies I inherit a lot of money and the house for life. I am not looking forward to my inheritance.

Darby is five and the cutest button of a girl I have ever seen. She is a mix of Loreleis Caucasian and her father Ricks Latino DNA. She is also my God Daughter. A title I take seriously. She plays with her toys on the kitchen floor. I can hear her dolls conversing. The silly and childish arguments between them make me smile and break the kiss.

You okay Jordan asks.

I smile harder and flap my hands. I point towards the kitchen. Jordan listens and then smiles. She understands.

Shes so cute she says.

I nod.

And youre so sexy she whispers.

I shrug. Its true.

Jordan laughs and slaps my arm.

Im glad to make you happy she says. I worry about you so much. I hate that you have to go through this.

I feel this conversation is leading to Miki. I ease against her and we stretch out on the couch. In each others arms. My head on her shoulder and her hand rubbing my bare arm sticking out of my maroon school polo. Her touch feels so good that I purr.

I dont know how I would handle it Jordan says. If one of my brothers was in a coma. Not knowing when he would wake up.

Jordan has three older brothers. Way older. All three are jerks. They joke about homosexuality a lot. They throw the word fag around. They adopted this behavior from her superior mother. Jordan does not get along with them. Most of the time she avoids them and when she is with them she keeps quiet. She comes off as submissive which is how they expect women to be in her family.

I would have so many questions in my head Jordan says. What was she doing in a house filled with illegal guns. Is she a criminal. Did she kill that ATF agent.

I sputter my lips. Miki would never shoot anyone let alone a ATF agent. Not unless she had to. But I doubt it came to that. I am sure the FBI and all the other alphabet agencies know who killed the agent by now. They have the science. The science will prove it was not Miki.

You know Jordan said. Its okay if she killed him. If she was part of the gun thing.

I jerk my head off her chest and flinch. Is she out of her mind. Jordan has no idea what Miki does for a living. No one does. The world has no clue about Tenebrous and what they do. Would she say those words if she knew about Tenebrous. Should I tell her. No. Its not her business. That is for Miki to tell her and if she were here she would not say anything. She will have to live with this bit of ignorance.

Why was she there Jordan whispers. Do you even know.

I shrug and avoid her eyes. Usually I can swim in them for hours. Something I rarely do with anyone. But not now. Not when she is asking me questions that fill me with nausea.

I nod and shrug.

Can you tell me she asks. Her face innocent and anxious.

I shake my head.

Disappointment consumes her face right after a flash of anger. Jordan sighs.

Okay she says.

Darby sweeps into the room. A doll in each hand. Arms in the air. Dirty blond hair inherited from her mother in a sloppy pony tail. A smile on her shining face.

Time for dinner Aunt Prudy she cheers.

• • • •

Miranda sits on the other side of the bed and holds Mikis hand. They have known each other for years. She is a few years older than Miki and always wears a colorful conservative dress to match the tiny crucifix around her neck. She quietly prays to Jesus for Mikis return and her soul. I slouch over in the other chair and hold her other hand. I do not pray. I am not religious. I am spiritual. Miranda is okay with that. She makes snide remarks about other people not believing in her God. Sometimes she lightly polices us. In fairness her friends make reverse remarks to her. Miranda accepts people. She does not try to change us. She accepts me and my homosexuality. Miranda is part of my family. She is a psychic too. She can remove her consciousness from her body and go anywhere. She can see anything even if it was in a securely locked room. But like Miki and the others steel and concrete gives her a hard time. Miranda is also on Mikis Tenebrous team.

I should have been with her Miranda says.

She wipes her tears with a tissue from the box next to Mikis bed. She avoids my eyes. I avoid hers. I nod to her comment. Gray who also works with Miki said the same thing. Why were they not with her in that house in St Pauls. They always work together. They confronted Ruby Stahl for answers. She told them that Gray and Miranda were not needed. The job was not that dangerous at the time. Miki was to find the girl with the rare talent and report to Ruby. Miki was not to confront the girl. The Tenebrous would take care of the rest.

It didnt go as planned Ruby said and I feel just as shitty as you do.

I am not mad at Ruby. I believe her. I am not even mad at the crazy psychic girl who did this to her. The crazy girl who is still out there running free. I am sure she will not come back. She will not try to kill Miki. The cops and the federal agencies and Tenebrous are searching for her. She should be buried deep in the underground. If that is even possible anymore in this world of cameras on street corners and on front doors of houses and in businesses.

I drop into the ether. Into the net. And call my phone. After putting it on speaker I say in my unisex voice

You could be dead or in a coma too.

Miranda shrugs and says with a soft slightly southern accent Maybe. Either way I wouldnt mind. As long as Jesus was holding my hand while I was there.

She smiles at me from across the bed. Maybe she thinks her Jesus is holding Mikis hand where ever she is at. Maybe Miki is in a good place while she waits for her body to heal and catch up with her soul.

Maybe I am wishful thinking.

• • • •

Friday night. Lorelei and Darby sleep with Rick in their apartment. They do this every Friday night now. Sometimes Saturday night too. The first few weeks they started living here were tough on them. Lorelei missed her husband

and Darby needed her father. I suggested that they spend time with him. Spend a night at home. I am going to be sixteen soon. I am old enough to sleep in the house alone.

When I told Jordan about this she bounced in excitement.

I can sleep over she said. It can be like we live together.

I liked the idea. Lorelei did not. Sort of. She crossed her arms and covered her face with suspicion.

I dont know she said. She is your girlfriend. Would Miki be okay with this.

I nodded. I shrugged. I had no idea. But what could go wrong. Girls sleep over each others houses all the time at my age. Lorelei should not worry because we are a couple. Jordan and I love each other and we had already been together like that before. Nothing new would be going on. If it did. Plus it was not like a boy sleeping over. I could not get pregnant.

Lorelei thought about it for a few days. She decided to try it for one night. If Jordan slept over that would be okay. She felt better that someone would be with me in this big house.

Or I could call Miranda to come and sleep over Lorelei said. She can be with you.

I cross her arms and glared at her as if she had ten heads.

Lorelei laughed.

Darby offered to sleep here with Jordan and me. We could have a slumber party my God Daughter said. My eyes widened. The idea frightened me to the core. I shook my head.

Oh Lorelei said. I could go for that. Rick and I hadnt had a night alone in ages.

But like I said. Darby needed her dad.

Jordan and I order pizza and buffalo wings and watch movies. Since our tastes differ we each pick a movie. She searches the cables movie menu and finds a romantic comedy. I bring down from my room Hideo Nakatas clever crime film that plays around with time called *Chaos* which I never showed her. She should be into it despite the subtitles.

You learn any Japanese she asks as we cuddle on the couch. You watch so many of these films.

I shake my head. With so much school work and daily social pressure I might learn it after graduation. Maybe if I go to college I will study it.

Youre so smart Jordan says. Youll probably pick it up fast. I can barely pass Spanish.

I sense a bit of self pity in her voice. I smile into her dark eyes. She smiles back. I lightly kiss her lips and tap her heart.

I love you too she says.

I suddenly feel the urge to consume her. To hold her deep. She is not close enough to my soul. I kiss her again. Deep. Fast and hard. My fingers work under her t shirt from her hip. If Jordan thinks I will move to her bra she assumes correctly. My fingers caress up her smooth skin to the bottom of her bra.

Jordan stops my hand over her shirt.

No she says. But not in a playful way. She usually flows with my advances unless she had her period. She just finished one last week and mine was not for another two. Maybe she is kidding around. I tickle her sides. She squeals and tells me to stop. She worries I will make her pee her pants.

I hoover her. Almost straddle her. Her laugh infects me. Makes me laugh. Both hands work her sides. She tries to grab them.

Please stop she begs through her laughter.

I stop but my hands remain on her. I want the sexy mood back. I bring my fingers to her breasts. I intend to cup over her bra and see how she responds. I feel metal at the top of the cup. Like something pinned to it.

Jordan swats my hands away and pushes me off. She hugs herself and reddens with shame.

I drop back into my phone.

What is that I ask.

Nothing. Its nothing.

It is something I say. Tell me. I will not laugh.

Laugh she mutters and looks to the ceiling. No you will definitely not laugh.

I do not understand I tell her.

I should go Jordan says and stands. I cant do this.

I follow her across the room and grab her arm.

Do not go I say through the phone in my other hand. What is wrong. I am sorry.

No Jordan says. Dont be sorry. You did nothing wrong. I did. I screwed up. I knew it wouldnt work. Jordan reaches into her shirt through the neck and takes out the short narrow metal stick. It is a recording device. A sneaky one. Miki uses them for her work. So do government agencies.

Were you recording our conversations I ask.

Not me Jordan says.

My brain spins like that wheel on the television game show.

Raymond wants you to record me I ask.

Jordan nods.

And you said yes I ask.

She releases a sob into her hands.

Im so so sorry Jordan cries.

Feeling short of breath I tell Jordan to leave my house. Can you forgive me she asks as she walks to the front door. I am too distraught to answer her.

• • • •

Anger kicks me out of the house. It fuels my legs to walk fast. It also extinguishes my fear of the approaching night and the fact that I am walking alone through the city. I pump my legs all the way to Newark Avenue. Down the hill. Pass Harsimus Cemetery. Avoid the turn to my school and all the way to Jersey Avenue where I turn right. Straight to Medical Center. Why my sister is not staying at Christ Hospital which is a few blocks from our house will be a mystery to me. Not so deep a mystery compared to why Jordan betrayed me for her FBI stepfather. Jordan who I trust with my psychic ability. Jordan who I love.

I enter the hospital as visiting hours end. A small crowd occupies the lobby of the newish building. Stand around. Talk. Prepare to leave for the night. I focus on the elevator and sweep by anyone in authority that could question or stop me. Normally I would need a paper badge declaring me a visitor. Whenever I previously received one I always shoved it in my pocket. No one cares if a girl my age walks around here. I threaten no one.

I take the elevator up to the third floor. As I step out a group steps in. One white lady cries. Distraught about who she visited. The man with her rubs her back and says He will be all right.

I turn the corner. The nurses station is farther down from Mikis room. Softly and quickly I move to her room. My eyes on the quiet station. No one comes in or out. I hear voices though. Someone laughs.

I enter Mikis room and release the breath I was holding. I ease the heavy wood door closed. A soft click of the latch. I turn to my sisters bed. The curtain blocks my view. A nurse must have left it like that to give her privacy. Not caring how loud my Vans sound on the polished surface I walk over and pull the curtain open. My heart nearly explodes at the site in front of my eyes.

Someone stands on the opposite side of my sisters bed. Dressed in tight black. Tight around the swell of her chest and hips. The woman also wears a black cotton mask over her mouth and nose and a blank black baseball cap with long blond hair tucked into it. She aims an automatic handgun at my sisters head. A gun extended by a silencer.

I scream.

The woman swings the gun in my direction. I duck behind the bed as she fires. The bullet plunges into the wall. She runs around the bed. To the door. I dive out from my crouched position and grab her leg. She falls forward. Flat on the floor. The gun still in her hand. I crawl up her back. My fingernails dig into her body. Still screaming. I grab her head and pound it to the floor. Over and over.

Male voices fill the room. Security guards invade. One pulls me off the woman. The other helps the woman up. Does he not see the gun. She elbows him in the gut. Punches him in the face. He stumbles off. She picks up her weapon and runs out of the room.

I shake the other guard off and step away. Mikis machines beep her vitals. Her body appears unharmed. No bullet holes in her. No discharge smoke in the air. No powder burns on her skin.

   I crawl onto the bed. I hug her. Tight. I will not let her go. I will not leave her. One guard radios in about what happened. He gives a description of the woman. The other asks me what happened. Who am I. Who was that woman. I do not know. All I know is that someone wants my sister dead. Someone so desperate they tried to do it at her most vulnerable moment. And that infuriates me to no end.

Sweetest Bite

He should have stayed upstairs.

Mike Mallory stood in the middle of the stairway. Coming from the third floor of the walk-up apartment building was no problem on the crutches. Going back up was another story. The hot windowless space that trapped bodily gasses and stenches of residents throughout the day caused him to pant and rub the gratuitous sweat from his brown eyes. His teeth gripped the two days worth of mail, trying not to scatter it down the stairs, as his nose flared to take in musky air.

I should dump this shit and come back for it later, he thought. Probably all junk anyway.

Though, he could try using his psychic ability to carry the mail. Maybe even lift himself up the stairs. What if someone entered and caught him in action? They would freak out. Or maybe press him to do tricks. Either scenario was shit. He never wanted to use his ability again.

"Mike," a sweet female voice behind him asked. "Are you okay?"

He cringed, then regretted it, worried that she might have seen his face. He knew the voice. He loved the voice. It was a voice that made him wish he was fifty pounds lighter, good-looking, and not have a head shaped by a cesarian section when he was born.

"Hey, Becky," he said, removing the mail from his mouth and spreading his best smile through painful discomfort. He leaned against the wall and controlled his panting, trying not to look like some stairway pervert. "What brings you here?"

The woman a few years shy of Mike's twenty-three giggled. Maybe on a normal person, the bad lighting and sweat on her face would have distorted such a smile but Rebecca Tideland was blessed with a delicate bone structure that could never be ruined no matter what the circumstances. Plus, her body was always accentuated by the tight tops and skirts she wore. Mike didn't even want to look at it. It always set him off.

"You're so funny," she said, stepping around him, stopping a few steps ahead of him. "Do you need help?"

"Nah. I'm fine."

"You've had that horrible cast on for a few months," she said, motioning to it. "Shouldn't they take it off by now?"

"They wanted to but I like it so much I've been avoiding the doctor."

Becky frowned and tilted her head to the side, making her braided bangs move with it. Even in her confusion, she was beautiful. Guilty for messing with her, Mike quickly said:

"Next week. The doctor said next week."

The smile returned. Confusion vanquished.

"C'mon," she said, taking the mail from his thick hand. "Let me help you."

Becky, with her back to him, walked up to the landing that divided the first and second floors. He couldn't move, too entranced by her butt wrapped in that yellow skirt. She caught him staring and cleared her throat.

"Coming with me?" she asked, a little too damn throaty.

Mike Mallory rolled his eyes, gripped the crutches, and pushed himself up the stairs, wishing he could come with her.

• • • •

Each floor had four apartments. Mike lived across the hall from Becky. The other two neighbors never came out of their residence, or Mike never crossed paths with them. He was fine with that. As long as Becky was his neighbor. Forever. Even better, she could be his roommate in his one-bedroom apartment.

Mike, although friendly to strangers, was not much of a people person. Before Tenebrous recruited him, he spend most of his adult life bouncing from one retail job to another where he always had to perform to high company standards so his bosses made money. He hated it. It paid shit. He also hated warehouse and janitorial work even though it paid slightly more. He would have loved an office job. A sit-down job. He heard from co-workers in the past about how temp agencies could help him find that kind of job. Mail room work sounded interesting and easier on his bulk. That was before Ruby Stahl from Tenebrous entered his life.

"Here you are," Becky said as they stopped between their doors. An open street-side window blew in a light humid breeze. Holding his mail, she took her keys out of her purse. "Home sweet home."

Mike shook his head. Her voice sounded so confident using such corny words. Mike loved it. It made her more like girlfriend material instead of someone to mess around with once and a while.

"Thanks, Becky," Mike said, opening his door.

Inside his apartment, he turned to her. The door closed against his arm. Becky snuck a peek over his broad shoulder.

"How long have you been living here?" she asked.

"Almost four months."

"You think you'll buy some furniture?"

Mike shrugged. He didn't even know if he was going to live there anymore. Ruby Stahl found him this apartment. Tenebrous paid for it. They promised to pay for everything in his life until he got up to speed.

"I'm picky," Mike said.

"You do work, don't you?" she asked, tilting her confused head to the side again. "Before you got hurt you never seemed to be around."

Mike was training in New York when he moved in. Sometimes he spent ten hours in that damn room prepping his telekinesis for Tenebrous, Ruby Stahl, and Miki Radicci. A lot of good training did for him and them.

"It's kind of up in the air right now," Mike said. "Thanks again for your help."

Mike opened his mouth for the mail. Giggling, Becky shoved it between his teeth. He wiggled his eyebrows goodbye and closed the door as she opened hers.

• • • •

What Mike Mallory didn't have in his apartment he didn't need. He had a black leather reclining chair in the center of the living room, a wide-screen television posted to the wall, a queen-size mattress in the bedroom, and a refrigerator full of food thankfully delivered every week. The Tenebrous-issued laptop and cell phone were in the corner, behind his back, out of his sight unless he went to the bathroom. He had no use for those two items.

All was perfect. Night after night since he broke his leg he'd been doing the same things. He had no need to leave the house.

Not like the doctor recommended it. Sure, he had to walk around a bit but resting his broken leg was the top priority.

While watching one of the *Alien* sequels in the dark room, Mike finished his second can of beer. He needed maybe one or two more to feel a serious buzz even though he took a painkiller for his leg that always throbbed at night. Did the doctor really set the bone back together with metal or was the operation all show? Mallory would find out in a few days when the doctor took his x-ray and declared him ready to walk without the cast.

Anyway, he needed another beer. Now. But the kitchen area was across the room. Why he forgot to position the chair next to the refrigerator when he moved in he would never understand. No, he understood. Back then he thought he was invincible with his psychic ability. No one could hurt him. That damn Ruby Stahl instilled how special he was for his telekinesis. Mike, like a fool, fell for it.

He was a fool no more. And he was not lazy.

Mallory pulled the lever on the side of the chair and eased his legs down. He grabbed the brace off the floor and wrapped it around his throbbing limb. God damn, it was a bitch tonight. Had to be the humidity. Or was the beer working against the painkiller? Maybe that's why you weren't supposed to mix them.

With one more strap left to go to secure his leg, Mallory fell back in the chair and caught his breath, easing the pressure created by his large belly. Maybe he didn't need a third or fourth beer. Maybe she should use his ability to open the refrigerator, take out the beer, and float it over to his hand like he had done a million times before. Before he fucked up.

"Shit," he muttered, still not sure what to do, still not wanting to do anything.

A knock at the door.

Mallory flinched. People had to be buzzed into the building. Did someone sneak through the main door as someone exited? He had no friends in Jersey City. Or at all, lately. Mike smiled. Maybe it was Becky across the hall. She needed help opening a jar of pickles or wanted a cup of sugar?

Mike's appearance became apparent. He wore black boxers and a white t-shirt stained with tomato sauce from the mozzarella sticks he had delivered with his cheese steak. A cheese steak full of onions that blended well with his body in need of a shower two days ago.

"Uh, who is it?" he called out.

"It's me, Mike," a female voice said. Definitely not Becky.

He deflated and ignored the anger simmering in his soul.

"I'm not home," he called out. "Go away."

"C'mon now," she said with a slight southern lilt. "Open the door."

Mike grabbed the remote from the saddle pocket built into the side of the chair and turned up the volume right as a pack of aliens attacked the remaining soldiers trapped on their planet. She continued to knock over the machine guns, screams, and thumping music but her voice was gone.

A moment later, the door opened. Ruby Stahl entered and closed the door behind her. Mike threw his hands into the air and pressed the mute button on the remote. The woman in her mid-sixties wore jeans and a maroon hoodie that had to be uncomfortable in the current weather. Her short blond and white hair framed a smiling pixie face.

"What did you do?" he asked, gratuitous with annoyance. "Pick the lock?"

"I could have but I only did what I trained you to do," she said, shrugging, shoving her hands into the hoodie pockets.

Mallory remembered. Ruby Stahl had the same psychic ability as him but tenfold. She trained him how to use his in certain situations. In ways he never considered. Like moving the metal inside a lock.

"What do you want, Ruby," Mike grumbled. "I'm not in the mood for visitors."

"I wanted to check on you," she said, wandering the space in front of him, blocking the television. "You're hurt. You're family."

"I'm hurt but I'm not family," he said. "And I'm fine."

After peeking out at Communipaw Avenue, Ruby settled against the white window sill and blocked the somewhat cool breeze that Mike had been enjoying all night. He planned on buying an air-conditioner before he got hurt. Now, even if he ordered one online, how would he install it? Without using his damn ability?

"I sense bitter in your voice," she said.

"No shit."

"I guess that sort of explains why you don't return my calls on both of your phones." She glanced at the Tenebrous-issued phone on the floor. "Is the one I gave you broken?"

"Shit, I don't even think it's charged."

"What if I needed you for an assignment?"

"You would have me work in this condition?" he asked. "I might as well go back to retail and stand behind a register with this leg. Besides, you can live without me for a while. Whatever I can do, you can do ten times better."

"True."

Mike flinched. The single word, although said casually, stung him.

"Yeah, well," he said. "You can leave now."

"Have you visited Miki?" she asked.

"Do I look in any condition to go out to the hospital and traipse around?"

"I could drive you," she said. "I can get you a wheelchair."

"No, thanks."

"You're avoiding her?" she asked, her hands tapping away on the window sill.

Mallory stole a glance at her. He read no accusation on her face. Yet, he still felt guilty.

"I visited her," he said.

"Yes," she said. "You did. The day before you were released from the hospital. Almost two months ago."

Her words pushed him down even lower. Anger rose to shield him.

"I would like you to leave now unless you have something to say that has nothing to do with Miki," he said.

"Well," she said, rising off the sill to pace behind him. "I do. The agents will probably contact you but we discovered you and Miki are no longer suspects in the Aurora Blake investigation."

"They found that psycho?"

"No. They don't even know where to start looking for her."

"But you do?" he asked, a little doubtful.

"We found her before," she said. "You and Miki did."

"Yeah, that was fortunate," he said, pointing out his leg cast. "So that's it. They believe the story that Miki and I were walking down the street when we heard a gunshot? We bravely went to the house and made sure everyone was okay but instead were taken hostage?"

"Based on the evidence, they have no choice," Ruby Stahl said. "You both have clean records. Well, no convictions. Miki had a few arrests. But still, along with the fire burning almost everything away except for the basement full of weapons, they have nothing on you two."

Ruby, from behind, patted his shoulder.

"That's it," she said. "So you're getting your cast off in a few days?"

"Yeah," he said, shrugging her hand off. "Thursday."

"I hope you answer your phone. If I have work for you."

"Listen, Ruby. Don't call me." He took in a deep breath. "I'm done. I want out."

"Out of Tenebrous?" she asked, coming around the chair to stand in front of him. Her face was relaxed, unreadable.

"Yeah," Mallory said. "I know you did a lot for me and I appreciate it. When I find a job I'll pay you back."

"It's not about the money," she said. "It's about you. Are you quitting because of what happened?"

"I'm not quitting," he rasped. "I'm…I don't belong. I'm not like you people."

"You are our people," she said. "Don't ever forget that. Even if you were not with us, you're still one of us. That will never die."

"Whatever."

"Miki will be disappointed," she said, shoving her hands into her hoodie pockets.

"Miki doesn't feel anything," he mumbled. All because of me, he wanted to add.

"You don't think she'll wake up?"

"I pray to God, or whoever, every day she wakes up," Mallory said, pressing his fingers into the armrests. "Every damn day, I hope she doesn't die."

Ruby walked to the door.

"Don't make up your mind yet," she said.

She opened the door wide and revealed the couple outside across the hall.

"Oops, sorry," Becky said, giggling her embarrassment.

Mike saw her in the arms of some white dude wearing low-hung jeans and a hockey jersey that failed to cover his tight black boxer briefs peaking out. He had to be on drugs since his dirty blond hair was braided in rows to his scalp, and he scowled despite having the most beautiful woman in his arms. For a second, Mike and Rebecca's eyes met. He hoped to God she didn't see the hurt in his. Or, notice he was in his underwear.

"Fun building," Ruby said, glancing over her shoulder at Mike.

She exited the apartment, closed the door, and left Mallory with his pity.

· · · ·

Even though he didn't require the cast on his leg anymore, the doctor said he would need a cane for a short while. When he stood off the exam table and applied pressure to both his legs, only the good one held him up. The formerly broken one was so weak it made him lean into the exam table. The doctor told him not to worry. After a few weeks and with lots of walking, his leg will return to normal.

On his way home, he stopped at the pharmacy to order a cane. Thankfully, the insurance Tenebrous issued him paid for it. Ruby hadn't cut him off yet. Or, would she even do it? She seemed so sure he was going to stick with them even after his disastrous first assignment.

Using one crutch, Mike hobbled back to his building, up the three flights of stairs, and into his apartment. He did okay. He found it easier going up the stairs. But he was as exhausted as if he were still wearing the cast.

Settled in his chair with the television on, he ordered dinner and caught his breath. Another cheese steak with onions and mayonnaise arrived. He settled on a movie and ate his dinner. The evening went quietly. Predictably. He grew bored. When he was bored, he felt a little horny. He hadn't been with a woman in… Well, he didn't want to think about it, it had been so embarrassingly long.

Someone knocked on the door.

"Mike," a shaky and frantic female voice asked. "Please, be home."

"Hold up," he said, pushing his weight out of the chair. He knew the voice but never heard it in such distress. He was thankful he still wore his jeans and t-shirt and didn't strip into his underwear for the night. "I'm coming."

"Please, hurry," she said.

With no support, Mike moved with wobbly legs to the door. After a few steps, he grabbed the knob and opened it.

THE SENTINELS 27

Becky, wearing the tightest and shortest low-cut dress he had ever seen on a woman, stood in the hall. Her frightened and tear-filled eyes divided between Mike and the hallway.

"Please," she whined. "I need to come in."

"Uh, yeah. Of course."

Becky swept in and slammed the door behind her, taking Mike, who still used the knob as support, with him. He fell into it and managed not to shamefully fall on his ass. She pressed her manicured finger to her lips. Mike read her clearly and kept quiet.

A fist pounded on a door in the hall. Becky peered through Mike's peephole. Her hands clasped together and her breathing slowed. Mike watched her, straining on his good leg, wishing he could sit down.

"Becky," a man shouted. "Open this door." More pounding. "You hear me?"

A body collided and the man grunted. Becky jumped back from Mike's door and covered her mouth. Wood snapped in the hall. Mike scrunched his face in question at Becky. She urged him to be quiet. The man called out for Becky a few more times but his voice was now distant. Becky brought her eye to the door hole again. A few moments later, she released a deep breath and stepped away from the door.

"He's gone," she said.

"Who's gone?" Mike asked. "What happened? Are you okay?"

"I am now," she said, suddenly hugging him. "Thanks so much for letting me in. He was so mad, I literally feared for my life."

Mike, fighting through the tingles she released in his spine, wrapped one arm around her slight, shivering body. What he might do if he had two arms around her he didn't want to think about.

"Was it the guy I saw you with the other night?" he asked. "Your boyfriend?"

"Uh, huh. He got mad at me," she said, stepping out of his arm. "He has a short temper sometimes but he's mostly a pussycat."

Mike moved to the other side of the door, opened it a crack, and peeked at the damage outside. Becky's apartment door and part of the threshold hung open as if a wild beast plowed through it. He closed it, shook his head, and sighed.

"He broke into your place."

"It's okay," she said. "The landlord will fix it."

"Yeah, but don't you want to call the cops?"

"He's still on parole. I can't send him back to jail. Not for something I did. I shouldn't have spoken to that guy in front of him."

"What did you say to the guy that made your boyfriend so mad?"

"I thanked him for bringing my drink."

"Um, okay."

"He just needs time to cool off. We need some space until his head clears. It always helps him," Becky said. "Do you mind if I hang here a few hours?"

• • • •

THE SENTINELS

"Can I get you something to drink?" Mike asked, hobbling with his one crutch to the refrigerator. "I got water, Gatorade, beer."

"I could use a beer if you don't have anything stronger," Becky said, standing between the television and the lounge chair.

Mike nodded and opened the barren refrigerator. He took a can of beer from the shelf. Becky came over and grabbed it from him. He pulled another can for himself. They drank in uncomfortable silence.

"So you only have this chair to sit on, huh?" she asked.

"Sit down. Make yourself comfortable."

"Oh, no," she said, smiling and throwing her free hand at him. "You're the disabled one. You should sit. You look like you're going to drop."

"It has been rough," he said. Mike explained how one leg was stronger than the other. "But the doctor said it shouldn't last."

"You don't have to do physical therapy?"

Mike shrugged and said:

"He didn't mention it."

"Well," she said, smirking. "What are you waiting for? Go for it."

Mike's brows went up and his heart stopped a second.

"Excuse me?" he asked.

"Sit before you drop."

"You sure?"

"Yeah, I'm sure," she said. "You think I'm a heartless person?"

"No," he said. "I think you're a beautiful person."

Becky's cheeks blushed as she sipped her beer.

"Thank you," she whispered from behind the can.

Mike dropped into the chair and placed the crutch on the floor. Becky wandered the apartment.

"So when will the furniture be delivered?" she asked.

"I didn't order any. I might have to move. My job isn't working out."

She whipped around to him and gasped.

"Oh, no. Really?" she asked. "I like having you as a neighbor."

"I'll still be in JC. Maybe Bayonne." He shrugged and drank. "We can hang out."

"I'd like that," she said. "But I don't think Leo will."

"Leo the boyfriend?"

She nodded.

"Leo shouldn't be treating you like that. I would never get mad at my girl if she thanked a waiter."

"He has an insecurity problem. He's going through a rough time."

"I guess parole can do that to a man," Mike mumbled behind his can.

"You have a girlfriend?" she asked, stopping in front of him.

Mike tried not to look at her body in that dress. His sweatpants would fail to hide his appreciation.

"No," he said, shrugging.

"I'm shocked," she said. "You're so sweet. Plus, you're cute in a teddy bear kind of way."

"I hear that a lot."

Becky laughed.

"I bet you do." Words lulled. Silence took over. Drinks were sipped. "I don't like to sit on floors, not in dresses like this, do you mind if I sit a while?"

Mike grabbed the arms of the couch and started pushing his weight up.

"Definitely," he said.

"No," she said, holding her hand up to him, moving him back down without touching him. "I can sit on the side."

"Uh, okay."

Becky positioned her butt on the arm of the chair and crossed her legs over his one leg.

"That's better," she said.

Her breasts were at level with his eyes. If he looked down, he would be staring at her legs. Maybe this wasn't a good idea.

"Tell me more about if I were your girlfriend," she said.

Mike flinched.

"What do you mean?" he asked.

"You know what I mean," she said, smiling, sipping her beer. "I want to hear more."

"Why? What would it matter?"

"I'm curious."

Mike shrugged and glanced at the door opposite of her.

"I don't know," he said. "I'd treat you right. I'd respect you. I certainly would never go nuts if another guy talked to you because it was part of his job."

Becky slipped off the arm of the couch and her butt landed on his thigh. She giggled and kicked her legs.

"Oops," she said like a little girl.

Mike tried to laugh but his concentration was on another part of his body. A part he couldn't control.

Becky switched her beer to her other hand and slipped her arm around Mike's shoulders. Her face gravitated to his.

"You like me," she whispered. "I can feel it."

"I'm sorry." He squirmed, trying to ease her off so he could jump out the window and die. "I didn't mean it."

"No," she said, holding her place on his lap. "I like it."

Mike reluctantly chuckled, focusing hard on that door but not really seeing it.

"Why won't you look at me?" she asked.

Mike shrugged again. His throat was too dry to speak. Becky dropped her empty can on the floor and, pressing his chin, steered his face toward hers. Their brown eyes latched.

"That's better," she said. "Isn't this nice?"

He nodded, wading into the strange feeling her eyes filled him with.

"It could be nicer," she said.

Becky pressed her lips to his. Mike grunted to protest but then she slipped her tongue in. Their arms wrapped around each other as their mouths moved, tasted, and teased.

"I could get used to that," she panted, breaking off the kiss.

"So could...

Someone pounded on the door.

"Becky, you in there?" an angry male voice asked.

Shivering, she pushed herself into Mike who stared at the door with her. What was with this guy? How did he even think of checking his place for her? Mike couldn't imagine Becky bringing him up in conversation. Didn't matter, anyway. All they had to do was keep quiet. He wouldn't be so stupid to break in here as he did with her apartment.

"Go away," she shouted. "I don't want to see you anymore."

Panic jetted through Mike's veins. His eyes bugged. Was she insane? He pushed her off his lap, not caring if she landed on her ass. The erection in his jeans was no longer a problem.

Leo pounded again.

"You better open this door," he screamed. "I'm sick of your shit."

"If you don't get out of here," she shouted, standing close to the door, pointing at it, "he's going to beat your white trash ass!" She glared at Mike and asked, "Right?"

On his crutch and far from the door, Mike searched the floor for his cell phone. He must have left it in the bedroom. All he could see was the Tenebrous phone that needed charging.

"Maybe you should go talk to him," Mike said.

Becky gasped as if he asked her to do something outrageously unsanitary. The door burst open so hard that the top hinge broke off.

"Jesus," Mike shouted, appalled. "What the fuck is wrong with you?"

"Get out of here," Becky screamed, her face distorted by anger, frightening Mike more than Leo. "Or he's going to beat your ass?"

"This piece of shit?" Leo asked. "This slick, fat piece of shit who can't even stand like a man?"

"He's more of a man than you," Becky said. "He knows how to treat a woman. You're a fucking child compared to him."

"Listen," Mike said, holding a free hand up. "I think you should both get out of here. I made a mistake. I'm sorry."

Leo shot bullets out his eyes at Mike who noticed the scar that divided his one eyebrow and continued onto his cheekbone.

"You're going to be sorry," he said, stomping over to Mike. He kicked the crutch out from under him, sending Mike to the floor. Leo swiped the crutch and raised it high in the air. "You're going to be real sorry, fucker."

Mike glanced at Becky, hoping to see her attack her boyfriend. All he saw was the disappointment on her face, disappointment in him.

• • • •

A cop guarding the hospital room stopped Mike Mallory. Showing him the badge stuck to his shirt, Mike told him he was visiting Miki Radicci. Putting all his weight on his new cane, Mike took out his requested driver's license. The cop approved it, frisked Mike, and told him to go inside.

He found two others with Miki still in a coma. Ruby Stahl sat in a chair on one side of the bed, facing the entrance. Her face formed a question when she saw Mike. The other person across from her, her back to Mike, turned around. A teenage black girl with curly hair out like a sunset. She wore a pink t-shirt, black jeans, and Hello Kitty Vans. She too was curious about Mike. At first, he didn't place her, but then he remembered Miki talking about her.

"Mike Mallory," Ruby said. "This is Prudy Radicci. Miki's sister."

Mike stopped at the foot of the bed and nodded at the girl who avoided his eyes. Ruby stood and offered him her chair.

"Nah, I can't stay long," he said. "I only have a few minutes."

Ruby sat back down.

"You look like shit," she said, making Prudy guffaw and flap her hands. "You fall down the stairs?"

Mike nodded. When he assessed the bruises on his face and ribs, he thought the same thing. No way he was going to tell her about Leo beating him down. Nor about how Becky left Mike to bleed on his apartment floor.

"What's with the cop?" he asked. "You said we were no longer suspects."

"Still true," Ruby said. "But something happened the other night. Someone tried to kill Miki."

The room tilted. Mike grabbed the foot of the bed to keep steady.

"Who would want to kill her?" he asked. "The Blake girl?"

"We don't know," she said. "We do know that we're not going to leave her alone. Her *family* is not going to leave her alone."

Mike nodded. The world stopped tilting. He closed his eyes, sighed, and shook his head.

"It would be great if we had your help," Ruby said.

Prudy held Miki's limp hand. Miki's face appeared so serene. He hadn't known her too long but had never seen it that way before. It seemed wrong someone would want to kill a face so calm. If he protected her better, Miki wouldn't be in this position, in this room.

"Can you help us, Mike?" Ruby asked.

It took a moment but he gave her the answer.

YP Was Here

Though they were on the lower level of the brownstone and watching a loud thriller, they heard the front door slam. Raymond Resnick, on the couch in front of the television, and his wife Samantha glanced at each other. Aside from Jordan, they were the only three that lived in the spacious house a block away from the pristine Van Vorst Park on York Street. Her three older sons were either married off or shared their own apartments in New York. Samantha liked how the house grew emptier. Raymond didn't.

Since marrying a woman with four children, he grew accustomed to having them in the house and learned to treat them as his own since their father died when Jordan was five. While Samantha sighed about how she wished they would all move out so she could enjoy peace, quiet, and marriage, he silently wished that they all stayed home to fill the house with life.

One time, he contemplated having a child with Samantha. She was forty years old when he brought it up. What a mistake he made. Babies were a lot of cleaning, playing, and feeding. Plus, the lack of sleep. She was too old to go through that again, let alone a pregnancy that would ruin the work she put into her body the last sixteen years. She had done it four times and that was more than enough. Raymond understood. How old would he be when the child turned twenty? In his early sixties. Would he even live that long?

"Jordan," Samantha, laying in Raymond's arms, called out. "Is that you?"

"Of course, it's me." Jordan stomped down the stairs, huffing with her arms crossed, her purple and orange backpack still on her shoulder. Despite the annoyance distorting her face, the teenager of Asian descent shared a lot of her mother's features.

"What are you doing home?" Samantha asked.

"Thought you had a pajama party," Raymond said.

Jordan's face dropped into disgust.

"Pajama party? Really?" she asked.

Raymond lightly smiled. Jordan was at that sensitive age where it was fun to rib her.

"Did you and that girl have a fight?" Samantha asked, straightening up on the edge of the couch, in full mom mode, and out of Raymond's arms.

Jordan opened her mouth to speak, then stopped. She glanced at Raymond, then her mom, and said:

"Something came up. She had to go out."

"Something to do with that sister?"

Jordan shrugged.

"I don't know. She didn't say."

"The girl can't say anything," Samantha said. "It's a wonder you spend any time with her at all."

"You should have called us," Raymond said. "It's a long walk. Plus, the time."

"The streets were busy," Jordan said. "It was no big deal. Can I go now?"

"We're watching a movie," Samantha said. "You can join us."

Raymond nodded.

"We can even find something you like," he offered.

"No, thanks," Jordan said. "I feel like being alone."

When Jordan went back up the stairs, Samantha returned into Raymond's arms. He pointed the remote at the television but waited to press the button.

"Something is up," Samantha said.

"Probably teenage stuff like we went through," Raymond said or hoped.

"No," she said. "It's that retarded girl. I don't like her. I always feel like she's hiding something from me."

"She's not retarded," Raymond said, smiling and shaking his head. "She's autistic. And, she can't speak, so that's probably why you feel like she's hiding something. You've always been suspicious of shy or introverted people."

"No, it's because her sister is involved with selling guns and murder," Samantha said. "Why is that not obvious to you?"

"Because her sister is innocent until proven guilty."

Samantha flashed her husband an incredulous look.

"You're another one," she said. "I think you know something about the investigation."

"How would I know something about it when I'm not a part of it?" he asked.

"You government agents are all talking to each other," she said, pressing harder against him, bringing her bare feet up on the couch. "Like a bunch of old ladies at a water cooler."

Raymond laughed, imagining her description. When Samantha said no more about the subject, he pressed the button on the remote and resumed the movie.

• • • •

Saturday morning. Raymond enjoyed the quiet in the house. Jordan was still sleeping and probably wouldn't wake up until noon. Samantha left early to play golf and eat breakfast with her friends at the Liberty National Golf Club. That left Raymond alone to sleep a little late, make a pot of coffee, and catch up on his email.

Wearing his favorite gray sweatpants and Mets t-shirt that he forbid Samantha to throw out even though it had tiny holes at the bottom and stained with deodorant at the pits, he sat in his home office behind the oak desk. The window behind him was open to let in the cool morning air and the sounds of neighborhood kids playing. One hand on the mouse and the other bringing the mug of coffee up and down to his face, he caught up on sports and current events on his home page.

Nothing in the current events held his interest. His concentration was off. Who was he kidding? He wanted to wake up Jordan and find out what happened between her and Prudy Radicci. He was sure that Jordan would catch something on the surveillance recorder. Yes, he knew the girl couldn't speak but she used an augmentative alternative communication device that could be recorded. If worse came to worse, Raymond could use any texts Prudy sent to Jordan's phone or notes that Prudy wrote down to Jordan. The investigation into Miki Radicci was desperate for anything.

Raymond stood out of the chair and stared at the open office door. He should walk right up the stairs to Jordan's room. This was official FBI business. It had nothing to do with family even though he was using his family. Then why did he hate himself so much? He hated using Jordan's secret against her. He would never tell Samantha that her daughter was a lesbian.

But Jordan couldn't chance it and that depressed Raymond the most. Jordan truly thought he would squeal to Samantha and break their trust as stepfather and stepdaughter. A trust he worked hard for all these years.

Raymond sat back down and sipped his coffee. He would wait. He would give her time. If something went wrong last night with Prudy Radicci, then Jordan would tell him.

His attention returned to his laptop, Raymond opened his email, hoping to distract himself with bills and correspondences. Instead, one spiked his annoyance. A message from his bank telling him that he was in danger of overdraft. How could that be? They had three times enough money for their monthly bills in their checking account.

Raymond clicked the link the bank email provided that would bring him to the issue on his account. Or, it should have done that. Instead, the screen went white and the little wheel at the top left of his browser spun clockwise, signaling that his computer was trying to connect with the page.

What the hell?

He Xed out of the screen and clicked the link again. And again, the white screen popped up and the wheel spun.

"Ray?"

He looked up from his laptop at Jordan standing on the threshold. She wore sleep shorts and a long t-shirt with her high school logo on the breast. Her long, straight dark hair hung wild from a lost sleep battle. Her face clean of make-up and dirty with depression disturbed him. He hadn't seen her like this since last year when she came out about that little bastard continuously raping her.

"Hi, Jordan," he said, trying to smile and hoping she would too. "Did you have breakfast yet?"

Jordan closed the office door and approached his desk. The only other chair was a heavy one against the wall. She stood in front of him like a guilty schoolgirl with her hands clasped in front of her. Her eyes focused on the window behind him.

"She knows," Jordan said. "Prudy found out about the recording thing."

She placed the tiny, narrow device on his desk. Tears started down her cheeks.

"How did she find out?" Raymond asked, taking the device and inspecting it as if he had never seen it before.

"I didn't tell her," she said, her voice rising in panic. "I swear. We were... She felt it. She found it. I didn't tell her it was for you. I swear. But she figured it out. She was so..." Jordan sobbed and covered her mouth with both hands. "She was so mad at me. She's never going to speak to me again, and I don't blame her."

Raymond closed his eyes and sighed, hoping to relieve the pressure around his heart.

"I'm sorry, Jordan," he said. "I didn't think it would turn out this way."

She pulled a tissue from the box on his desk and blew her nose. She shivered. He doubted it was from chills.

"Don't worry about it," he said, holding the recorder up.

"Are you going to..."

"I'm not going to say anything to anyone," he said. "And, um, I'm sure Prudy will speak to you again. You can tell her the truth. She has to understand. She loves you, right?"

She didn't seem relieved. Maybe she was too stressed out. Maybe the wound was too deep and fresh for any comfort.

"Feel like some butterscotch pancakes this morning?" he asked. "Still your favorite?"

Jordan nodded.

"That would be nice."

She left the office. Raymond inhaled deeply and fought the choking sensation. Yes, Prudy had to forgive Jordan. It wasn't her fault. It was her rotten stepfather's fault. Maybe he should go down to the Radicci house and explain it to the girl. But would that ruin the investigation into Miki Radicci even more?

Raymond brought his attention back to the bank email. The link still didn't connect. Instead, he logged into the bank website. It worked. He checked his account and saw no alerts. Actually, the checking account had as much money as he thought previously.

Stupid bank screw-up, he assumed. He checked his phone and saw they didn't send him a text alert even though he was signed up for them. Yes, it was another bank mess-up. The alert was for someone else with a similar account number.

Right?

Raymond closed the laptop and went downstairs to make his stepdaughter breakfast and comfort her heartbreak.

. . . .

Monday morning. Raymond, with a Dunkin Donuts coffee in hand, walked through the bull pit of desks and greeted the other agents settling in or gabbing. Without stopping, he made his way to his desk against the window that looked out to a large parking lot and a section of Newark. The sky was clear and the sunrise obscured his monitor. As always, he pulled the translucent shade down over the window behind his desk and logged into his terminal to check work emails.

"What the hell?" he rasped.

Porn site advertisements and foreign women wanting sex with him filled his work inbox. The blood dropped from his brain and pushed down at his heart. How the hell could this have happened on a secure government server?

"Hey, Jess?" he asked the agent two desks away from him. She picked apart a cruller and glanced through large-framed glasses at him. Raymond smiled. "Have a good weekend?"

She shrugged.

"Kids were ornery but I guess it was okay," she said. "This weekend should be better. Danny and I plan to go away to..."

"Um, anything weird with your email this morning?"

Her blond brows went up.

"Weird, how?" she asked.

Raymond smiled and tried to chuckle.

"Oh, weird email?" he asked.

"Nope. Business as usual," she said. "You okay, Ray?"

"Yeah, sure," he said, turning back to his terminal.

Jess shrugged and returned to her cruller.

Raymond scrolled down the inbox. And down. A hundred or more sex messages? A hacker. It had to be some psycho hacker. Somehow. But was it only his email that got raided like this? And, if so, why him? Did he mess up during a search? Or was his email on some darknet site?

Raymond picked up the desk phone to call IT when a new message popped up. The subject line read:

READ THIS OR SUFFER

Ray opened the email, reminding himself not to click any links or attachments. It read:

I know BonnieBrai100% is your password. You do not know me and you are most likely wondering why youre getting this email.

I placed malware on your computer. Your internet browser now operates as a RDP (Remote Control Desktop) which provides me with access to your screen and webcam. I also collected your entire contacts from your Messenger social networks and email.

What exactly did I do.

I made a doublescreen video. First part displays the pornography you were watching and the second part displays the recording of your web cam and you masturbating to the pornography.

What should you do.

2000 is a fair price for our little secret. Youll make the payment through Bitcoin.

BTC adress HEK24hS8UJ3577JklB

You have one day in order to make the payment. I have a specific pixel within this email and right now I know that you have read this email. If I dont receive the BitCoin I will send out your video to all your contacts including relatives and coworkers, etc. If I do get paid I will erase the video immediately. This is nonnegotiable.

YP

Raymond shook his head. It had to be a scam to scare him. No way someone had that kind of video on him when he never did what they claimed. Over ten years ago, an agent in Colorado was caught watching what he thought was pornography at home but it turned out to be child

THE SENTINELS

pornography. Somehow, the Bureau found out and that agent was now serving fifteen years. Since then, Raymond never took any chances and saved all his sexual thrills with Samantha or the occasional DVD.

No, this was bullshit.

Raymond checked the time and saw that he had a few more minutes before he had to report to his assignment. Just enough time to call IT and get this shit straightened out and off his computer.

• • • •

Raymond slumped over the desk in the dark windowless office. The only light came from the computer monitor and the desk lamp. His suit jacket hung on the back of the chair and his white sleeves were rolled up. The air failed to push through the vent again. He knew the air conditioning was on. He caught a cool sensation throughout the rest of the building. Nope. The air in this office had to be rigged to punish the occupant. Raymond felt punished. Punished for the last month.

When he started transcribing the surveillance recordings submitted by other agents, he only found a handful of short files in the cue. Raymond estimated he could finish by lunch. If all went well, he could catch up on his regular work piling on his desk.

The easy and fastest part was running the recordings through the AI program that changed the audio into words. The daunting part was listening to the tapes while reading the AI translation to make sure they matched. Sometimes the AI confused certain words. Foul words and phrases. Even other languages were a problem. Raymond's job was to translate what the stupid AI failed to figure out.

A knock at the door pulled Raymond away from the first MP3 file. Agent Linderman, followed by his excessive use of cologne, entered. The middle-aged man with cropped black hair that receded to the middle of his head and a pot belly that his suit jacket was never able to hide smiled and closed the door behind him.

"How was your weekend, Ray?" Linderman asked.

Ray shrugged.

"Okay, I guess."

"Did you do that thing we talked about on Friday?" he asked, lowering his voice.

The pain Raymond worked so hard to leave at home filled his chest. He pulled the narrow recording device from his breast pocket and handed it to Linderman. The other agent smiled, on the edge of excitement.

"It was a wash," Raymond said. "Radicci found it."

Outrage killed his stupid grin.

"That stupid girl," Linderman spat.

Raymond flinched. Linderman had better meant Prudy Radicci and not Jordan. He was one step away from punching the other agent out.

"How could she have found it?" Linderman asked. "Did your daughter say something?"

"No. She just found it."

"She had it pinned to her bra? The tech guys said that's the best place."

"She did everything you suggested. I'm sorry, it didn't work out."

Linderman deflated. Raymond felt a bit sorry for him. Agent Linderman and his partner had been working the case for months, trying to find something on Michelina Radicci and Michael Mallory. Unless they had some new, solid evidence, both suspects would be cleared for the murder of the ATF agent and all the other bodies in Aurora Blake's rampage through many states.

"Maybe the tech guys have something smaller," Linderman said. "The girl is retarded. How the hell did she figure it out?" A smirk stretched. "You don't think they...you know." He made a hole with his thumb and index finger and poked the middle finger of his other hand through it. "Or, however dykes do it."

"I got to get back to work," Raymond said, gripping the arms of the office chair and hoping they were strong enough not to rip out.

"We'll talk more later," he said, moving to the door.

"No. No more."

"What do you mean?" Linderman asked, stepping back to him. "We can't give up."

"You can't give up," Raymond said. "It's not my case."

"Ray, do I need to repeat what this will mean to you? Do you want to be punished forever down here?"

"Not if it means messing with Jordan's life," he said. "She's been through a lot this year. Besides, Radicci is not speaking to her. How would she even be able to get anything?"

"I don't need to know how she gets it," Linderman said. "You said they're good friends. She saw your stepdaughter's bra. Maybe she can...you know." Again with the lewd hand gesture. "Get in there."

"She's fucking sixteen and like a daughter to me," Raymond said. "Stop doing that with your hands."

Linderman held his palms up in supplication.

"Fine, Ray," he said. "No more. I won't ask for your help. I thought you could use this after the Trenton thing to get back on the ladder. I thought you were done sitting in this room proofreading and smelling your own farts all day. But if you change your mind, let me know."

Linderman left the room. Raymond jumped out of the chair and swung his leg to kick at the door. He stopped. If he kicked a hole in it they would probably make him pay for it out of his check.

After a few deep breaths to calm his body and mind, Raymond returned to the computer and where the tension returned. The cue was filled with 8 new MP3 files to translate.

• • • •

A cloud hung over the dinner table that night. Jordan barely ate the Chinese take-out Samantha ordered again and she answered all her mother's questions about her day with one word. Sometimes one syllable. While Samantha grew aggravated with her daughter, Raymond sunk into a depression. These two were on the borderline of a feud that wouldn't be resolved since Jordan couldn't tell Samantha the truth and Raymond would be the one responsible. Well, Linderman was to blame. Fucking Linderman.

Later, Raymond knocked on Jordan's door while Samantha made a few work phone calls. Soft rock music pressed against it. Raymond hoped it wasn't to cover her crying.

"Jordan?" he asked. "You have a minute?"

"Yes," squeaked out and the music stopped. Raymond opened the door and reluctantly smiled at her. The girl in her pajamas sat cross-legged on her mussed, soft pink bed and cuddled a large stuffed penguin on her lap. A solitary lamp on the night table performed a horrible job of illuminating anything.

"Was worried about you," Raymond said. "Wanted to see how you were doing."

Jordan shrugged, her mood no better than at dinner time.

"Did you see Prudy today?" he asked.

Staring at the bed, she shook her head and sniffled.

"She wasn't in school," she said. "And she won't return my texts or calls."

Raymond nodded and crossed his arms. His eyes avoided her sorry sight.

"Would you like me to talk to her?" he asked. "After all, I am to blame."

Jordan rubbed her eye with the heel of her hand as if trying to reach a pain deep in her head.

"No," she said. "I don't know. Don't."

Raymond nodded.

"I won't. Not unless you tell me to."

Since bringing anything else up would seem useless, he wished her a good night.

Still hearing Samantha bossing people on the phone downstairs, Raymond entered his office and turned on his laptop. He opened his email account and found the subject line TIME IS RUNNING OUT.

"No fucking way," Raymond said.

He opened the email. No message in the body but the letters YP. YP signed the previous email at work. Was that their name? YP? Was their first name was Yevgeny or Yelena? Was this a Russian hacker messing with him?

Raymond blocked and deleted the email.

Too aggravated with technology, Raymond went downstairs and searched for a movie to stream. With any luck, he hoped to wipe the rotten day from his nerves.

• • • •

The next morning in the Newark field office. Raymond, again with his coffee from Dunkin Donuts, made his way through the bull pit of desks. He smiled and greeted the other agents and employees. Some said good morning. Some smiled so hard that they broke into laughter. Some, mostly the women, scurried off as if he had Covid.

He sat at his desk and turned on his terminal. Jess, the agent two desks away glared at him. Raymond smiled at her, hoping she would stop making him feel like a piece of crap with her expression.

"Is there something wrong, Jess?" he asked, concerned, confused.

"Ugh," she sighed. Jess dropped her half-eaten cruller into her garbage and left her desk.

Raymond shrugged. He was not going to let her behavior bother him. If he offended her by accident yesterday, and, as far as he knew, he'd done nothing wrong, he would apologize to her later. He intended to have a good day today. A positive attitude.

THE SENTINELS

With the email program on, Raymond scanned down his list. The porn sites were gone. IT did a fine job, and he appreciated it. They too believed a hacker was flexing to their friends but they would investigate it further so it wouldn't happen again.

YOURE FUNERAL, a subject line read.

Raymond's body tingled and his peripheral vision flashed black and white. No, no. IT took care of the problem. How could this jerk still access his work email? He clicked on the message and found a shortened link. He placed the cursor over it, closed his eyes, and clicked it.

Thankfully, he always kept the volume off on the monitor. His eyes still closed, he prayed to God in his head. Please, please, let this be a joke. He opened his eyes and saw what YP promised him if he did not pay the BitCoin on time.

A split screen. On the left side a porn video. Nothing kinky or unsanitary. Only a man Raymond's age and a young Asian woman pleasuring each other on a nice couch in a brightly lit space that could have been a Florida beach condo. The other side of the screen had an average-built middle-aged man naked from the waist up. You couldn't see below where the man's hand was pumping away but the badly lit face was clearly shown. The man looked like Raymond. Looked! It couldn't be him. The background, what little was shown due to a lamp off-screen and focusing on the man's side, was nothing like his office at home. How could they have made this? Some kind of AI software?

A raucous laugh jolted his attention from the screen. Raymond couldn't find the laughter. He did see the other monitors facing him. A few played the same video. YP sent it to everyone!

Raymond stood, grabbing their attention. Some glared. Some snickered. Some frowned. Who was this man they always worked with who seemed so normal?

Raymond shook his head.

"That is not me," he rasped.

His cell vibrated on his desk. Samantha's name branded across the screen.

No, no, no.

He snatched it up and connected the call.

"Ray," Samantha cried out. "What is this?"

"Wh-what?" he asked.

"This video came in my email," she asked, her voice stuck between crying and raging. He hadn't heard her like this since Jordan's problem last year. "Why are you in this video?"

"That's not me," he said, loud enough for everyone to hear.

"Don't tell me it's not you," she screeched. "I know my husband when I see him."

His desk phone rang. Raymond picked it up. Before he could say the greeting all agents were supposed to use, a female voice said:

"Agent Resknick? Assistant Director Panera wants to see you in his office. Now."

He stumbled back and pressed against the window. Both phones in his hands and down at his sides.

"It's not me," he whispered, tears running down his clean-shaven cheeks. "I swear to God!"

Raymond tried to move his legs. Tried to report to Panera's office. Tried to explain that someone made the video of him. Tried to blackmail him.

His hands numbed, and he dropped the phones. Then his mind followed into unconsciousness. His body slumped down the window and tipped to the floor. Raymond would have to see AD Panera later.

Bless Me, Death

The middle-aged man wearing a dark gray suit and a shoulder holster under the jacket lay on the floor. A bullet hole was below his receding hairline of cropped black hair. Despite the cologne the dead man wore, it did nothing to mask the feces in his pants.

He knelt to the body in the second-floor hallway and, with leather-gloved hands, took out the dead man's wallet from the inside jacket pocket. The man's name was Joe Linderman. He was an FBI agent.

He closed his eyes, cursed in his head, and thought about his next move.

• • • •

It seemed like it was the last house to acquire. It wasn't. There were a few more in Jersey City. But this one was the most complex to buy. No. Resistant to be sold.

Richard Grossman sat in the driver's seat of his black BMW. The engine ran and the air-conditioner blew cool air onto his skin. He should have taken off his suit jacket before he drove out here. He would be sweating less even though he knew it had nothing to do with the weather.

From where he was parked on Booraem Avenue, the pale-skinned man in his mid-thirties with slicked-back hair observed the three-level Victorian house up on a slight hill to reveal its basement. An old black metal fence with hedges weaved through it lined the sidewalk and divided it from the neighboring properties. The welcoming wood porch and awning could use a paint job, as could the rest of the house.

The inside was nice. This he was sure of despite never entering it. It was recently renovated and cleaned up for the new residents. Or, the old residents. Radicci was still on the title but instead of Michael and Veronica Radicci who lagged on the mortgage payment and defaulted to the bank, it was Michelina Radicci who picked it up and paid it off.

Michael Radicci was assumed dead but since it was hard to prove it always complicated the sale of the house. Now his daughter Michelina Radicci was in a coma at Jersey City Medical Center across town. Richard Grossman read she was involved with some hostage situation on St. Paul's Avenue, resulting in the house exploding and a dead body. Grossman's heart nearly exploded through his chest. What were the chances that Michelina Radicci would die? When he read the part where Michelina Radicci and her accomplice were still alive, he wished his heart did explode. All over the office.

Hope for Michelina Radicci's death still sprung eternal in his mind. The sister, Prudence Radicci, would inherit the house, as stated in the filed court documents. Richard Grossman, with the backing of GLM Property Management and Sales, was prepared to pay a mid-to-high seven-figure price. Extreme for an old house but worth it considering what was in the basement. Or, in the ground of the property.

When he arrived at the house that afternoon, Grossman witnessed the blond woman leaving right on time. With her pre-school-age daughter donning pigtails, they walked hand-in-hand down the street. The blond woman also carried a large, weighed down, reusable bag. Perhaps she was taking her daughter to the Janet Moore Park on the next block. Good. He talked to the blond woman before in the winter. He didn't want to stir suspicion by dropping another card with her again.

Grossman waited for a different, fresh, point of sale.

Around 3:30, two teenagers stopped in front of the house. One was a light-skinned black girl with thick sprouted hair and an Asian girl with long dark hair braided into a tail. They both wore maroon shirts and black leggings and carried backpacks. The two girls, holding hands, walked up the porch steps and entered the house.

Grossman turned off his car, picked up the folder stuffed with papers explained market values of houses like the one on Booraem Avenue, and left the car. The unusual Spring heat wrapped around him as he crossed the quiet city street lined with other old houses and hundred-year-old trees pulling sidewalks up with their growth.

On the porch, he rang the bell and stretched his best smile, revealing the whitest teeth cosmetic surgery accomplished. The door opened and the black girl laid eyes on him. He tried to connect with hers but she was too focused on either his body or face. The Asian girl behind her met Grossman's eyes, though. Thank some god for small favors.

"Hello," Grossman said, light and pleasant. "Is Michelina Radicci home?"

Prudy shook her head.

"I see." Grossman introduced himself and offered his car. Prudy accepted it and studied both sides. Her fingertips caressed the texture of the card stock and raised print. "Will she be home later today? Perhaps sometime tonight would be convenient?"

Prudy shook her head again, still focused on the card.

"I see. Are you her daughter?"

Prudy sputtered and shook her head.

"She's her sister," the Asian girl offered.

"Oh, silly me," he said. "Then this might interest you as well. Are you aware of the market value of your house?"

Prudy spaced out but the Asian teen seemed interested. Grossman pulled a sheet from the folder. It listed similar houses to theirs in the Hudson County area. The sale prices were circled in red.

"Keep in mind my company, GLM Property Management and Sales is prepared to offer three times more any of those amounts for this house?"

"Holy crap," the Asian girl said. "Are you serious?"

"Indeed."

Disinterested, Prudy handed the sheet back to Grossman.

"No, please," he said. "Keep it. Show it to Ms. Radicci, your sister, when she returns. If she is interested in selling, have her call me at the number on my card. Anytime. It's a private line."

Prudy nodded and closed the door.

Grossman returned to his car. Prudy Radicci's disinterest in money, unlike her friend, disturbed him. If only their personalities were switched. Based on Grossman's family history and business, that could be possible.

• • • •

A few months later. Late June. Grossman was again in his BMW with the air conditioning doing little to cool him down. The time on the clock read 1:28 PM. If all went correctly, Lorelei Collins, the blond woman taking care of

Prudy Radicci while Michelina Radicci was still in a coma, would be taking her daughter, Darby Collins, to the park down the street and, with even greater luck, a few errands.

Grossman didn't realize the date. Not until an email from the Board of Directors hit his work inbox. Not only was he responsible for buying the house but to make sure the property was still functional. Still strong. Still ready to be used at a moment's notice. The property was created over a hundred years ago and was accidentally used in the last year. Based on previous readings, the property was running at full potential as the other houses. But this was what the Board wanted. Despite the G in GLM Property and Sales meaning Grossman, he was not on the Board and only in the company due to nepotism.

1:30 PM and Lorelei Collins and her daughter exited through the gate. Hand in hand and with a bulky bag filled with snacks and drinks, they headed down the block to the park.

Grossman opened the glove box and took out the ring of keys to the house that he had made after the renovations. Hopefully, Radicci didn't change the locks in the last few months. Turning off the engine, he noticed someone standing on the sidewalk at the gate to the house. A middle-aged white man with cropped dark hair and a domed pot belly sticking out of his open suit jacket. Grossman had no idea who he was but he sensed the man was an authority and arrogant.

The man walked up to the front door of the Radicci house and rang the bell. No one was home but the man didn't know that fact. He waited a few minutes and then entered the house.

Entered the house? A lock pick or key?

THE SENTINELS 59

Grossman sighed hard and hit the steering wheel. He had no time for this kind of delay. Maybe the man would be fast and Grossman could make up the time. He casually crossed the street to the house. He planned to head in the same direction as Lorelei Collins but stop at the corner of Palisade Ave. At that distance, he should see the man leave the house but far enough away to avoid suspicion.

He turned in front of the gate, when...

A gun popped in the distance.

From the house?

Grossman walked back to his car and entered it. A moment later, a tall slender woman in black pants and a black t-shirt exited the gate. Her long blond hair hung down over the sides of her face. He couldn't make her out unless she walked towards Palisade. She didn't. She headed towards Baldwin Avenue where she disappeared from his sight. He assumed she turned the corner. But then a motorcycle started up, and the woman with her blond hair sticking out of the sleek helmet drove off on it.

Who was this woman and where did she come from? He had been watching the house for an hour. Did this second person hide in the house until the Collins woman left? No. She must have been waiting on the other side of the house and broke in through the back door.

And whose gun went off?

If this blond woman had one, she was hiding it well considering nothing suspicious bulged out from her tight-fitted clothes. If she was unarmed, then it had to be the man's weapon. But where was he now?

Grossman hit the steering wheel, closed his eyes, and cursed. This was not happening.

But it was.

He had to do his job.

• • • •

What reason did Agent Linderman have to break into the Radicci house? Or, for the blond woman on the motorcycle to do the same? No way they were interested in the house. No one but the Board knew about what the property could do or its history. And if they knew, they probably assumed it was fantasy and silly. No. These two intruders were here because of Michelina Radicci. But what business did they have with her?

Grossman decided to think about it later. Lorelei Collins should be home in less than an hour and maybe Prudy Radicci, too. He couldn't let them find the body here. He couldn't let the cops cause any disturbance in the house. He and the Board of Directors had gone through so much to reach this point. The carrot was almost in their hands.

Grossman went down to the kitchen and gathered a bucket filled with hot soapy water, a few plastic bags from the market, and a scrubbing brush. Back on the second floor, he sealed Linderman's head in the plastic bags to keep the rest of his brains from spilling out. He dragged it a few feet from the mess it made and viewed no fresh smear.

He scraped his black gloved hands against the wood floor to scoop up the skull matter and dump it in the bucket of hot sudsy water and did the same for the spatter on the wall. Then, he scrubbed the floor and walls. Fifteen minutes later, he stood, panted, and accessed his work. Thankfully, the Radicci's never installed carpet or laid out floor rugs. Grossman nodded at his fine work. As long as the cops didn't use special lights to detect blood residue then no one should suspect someone shed their mortal coil in the hall.

Grossman dumped the red sudsy water in the bathroom sink down the hall. After cleaning the sink, the scrub brush, and his gloved hands, he placed the bucket and brush in the back corner next to the toilet. Its placement shouldn't cause too much suspicion to the residents. If he had time after moving the body to the backyard and hiding it until tonight to collect it, he would return the bucket to the kitchen.

Back in the hallway, Grossman gripped Linderman from his armpits and steered his bulk to the stairs. His back strained from the overweight agent. Dread and aggravation fought for control of Grossman.

The front door creaked open and closed hard. A female voice filled the air and nearly stopped Grossman's heart.

• • • •

"No," the woman's voice said from the downstairs hall. "Wash your hands first, then you can go watch TV."

Manic feet pounded hardwood. Moving farther away from his ears, heading to the bathroom next to the kitchen.

Grossman opened the bedroom door across from the stairs. Ignoring the *Hello, Kitty* shrine and massive movie collection, he saw a gap between the bed and the floor too narrow for the body to fit. Also, the sheets and blanket barely reached the box spring.

The other bedroom across from it was a bit sparse but clearly occupied by the little girl. Cute unicorn sheets and a blanket covered the mattress. Although the blanket did not reach the floor, a matching skirt for the box spring did. Grossman pulled it up and saw enough room. He dragged the body into the bedroom and shoved it under the bed. Sitting on the floor, he pushed it with his legs to make sure it reached all the way to the other side to avoid detection. He met resistance where the shoulder stuck out from under the bed. After a few more shoves that accomplished nothing, Grossman stood and pulled the bed out to see what was causing the resistance.

Someone had placed a bomb with a timer under the bed.

• • • •

No, no, no.

Not good at all. This house could not be blown up. The blond woman on the motorcycle must have left it here. Thankfully, Grossman found it in time. The timer had ten more hours to go.

Back on his feet, wiping the sweat from his face with a handkerchief, and gripping explosive device, he assumed the body would be safe for a few hours.

Should he sneak out of the house now and come back for the body later? That was the question blazing through his mind. The front door was the only option but a dangerous one. If the little girl or Lorelei Collins spotted him, Grossman would have to kill them. And what if Prudy Radicci caught him leaving as she was coming home? No. He had enough problems. He would have to wait this out.

Grossman inspected the third bedroom. A master bedroom and clearly used often. He went up the stairs to the third-floor space with a kitchen, an office with a couch, and a bathroom. He checked the toilet and found a rust stain around the inside of the bowl and a few dead bugs. No one had used it in a long time.

With the lid down and his butt on it, Grossman sat with his head in his hands and patiently waited while the explosive device the size of a VHS tape counted down in his hand.

• • • •

From the activity in the house, Grossman discovered some interesting facts that might be important to the sale of the house. He took breaks from the third floor and, when he felt confident and with his shoes off, sat on the stairs to the second floor where the house funneled voices into the hall. Based on conversations between Lorelei Collins and her daughter, Prudy Radicci wasn't expected home until dinner time. No, Prudy was not in school. She was at the hospital with Aunt Miki, remember?

Did something happen that Prudy Radicci stopped her meager high school education to focus on her sister? Was Michelina Radicci dying? One could only hope.

As planned, Prudy came home to eat and shower before going back to the hospital. Grossman hid in the third-floor bathroom while the disabled teen moved around her bedroom and the second-floor bathroom.

After the teen left, the mother and daughter settled down for a few hours of television and laughter. At 8:30 the bedtime routine began. The child bathed in the second-floor tub. The door was ajar, and Grossman heard nothing about the empty bucket and scrub brush he left inside.

In her pajamas, the little girl bundled into the bed for her bedtime story. *Cinderella*, again.

"Something smells," the little girl whined, her voice carrying through the open bedroom door and into the hallway.

Grossman, standing at the top of the stairs, gripped the railing and held his breath.

"I don't smell anything, sweetie," Lorelei said.

"I don't like it."

"Well, maybe a mouse died."

"Blah!"

"Don't worry. It's probably in the walls if I can't smell it yet. Mommy will try to find it tomorrow, okay?"

Grossman exhaled, slow and steady.

Kisses and goodnights were exchanged, and the mother offered the girl sweet dreams. Footsteps went down the stairs.

Grossman, holding his shoes and the bomb, soft-stepped to the second floor and listened. Laughter from a sitcom and a chuckle from the woman. Should he chance an escape now? Could he avoid a squeaky plank from the floor or keep the heavy door from scraping wood as it opened?

Bare feet padded in his direction. Grossman rushed back up the stairs on jerky legs trying not to add pressure to the wood. Lorelei Collins turned off the first-floor lights and walked between the master bedroom and the bathroom to prepare for sleep. The master bedroom light went off but the door was open to allow any sounds of distress from the daughter who also had her door open.

THE SENTINELS 65

Grossman, now in the dark hallway, stood and waited. He could escape through the back door of the house and take care of the explosive device. But the little girl noticing the smell of the dead body under her bed bothered him. Children were spoiled. What if she woke up in the middle of the night and demanded her mother check under it? What if the little girl investigated and screamed, thinking there was an intruder or a zombie hiding under it?

He had to remove the body and hide it in the backyard now until it was safe for his people to dispose of it.

But how?

A joyful charge shocked through his body, urging him to snap his fingers or stomp the floor, not realizing the actions would ruin his great idea.

• • • •

With his shoes in his hands, Grossman stepped onto the first floor of the house. He squeaked a few steps going down but no one came out to investigate. Thankfully, parent- and childhood wore people into deep exhaustion. Something he would know nothing about or care to experience.

First, he opened the front door for the humid late Spring night and the chirping cicadas to wade in. He then searched the dark hallway for something heavy. The space was devoid of sentimental or artistic objects. Even framed pictures of the sisters and their family were absent. It was not a welcome space for visitors.

In the kitchen, Grossman found a metal hammer under the sink. With his black gloves still on, he left the bomb on the kitchen counter and carried the hammer back to the front entrance. He took a deep breath by a small, stain-glass window lined up with the first landing that separated the stairs leading up to the first floor and smashed it with the hammer. It took a few blows but he managed to create an attractive sharp pattern the size of a basketball.

"Darby!"

"Mommy!"

Grossman dropped the hammer and dashed deeper into the house. He snuck into a front room right at the threshold of the dining room and eased the door open a crack. With the old furniture and cardboard boxes piled around, he figured it was used for storage. Lorelei Collins should escape out of the house and avoid moving deeper into it. No way she would investigate a break-in with her child present.

"C'mon, now," Lorelei said. "Watch out for the glass."

"Someone broke the window," Darby Collins said.

"I know."

"Why is the door open?"

"I don't know, sweetie. But we'll let the police figure it out. C'mon."

When their voice carried from the front of the house, Grossman returned to the second floor where he dragged Linderman's body out from the child's bed and hefted him onto his shoulder in a fireman's carry. Oh, how dead bodies increased in weight!

As he crossed the front hall, he spotted Lorelei Collins and her daughter waiting at the black gate. The mother spoke on the phone. Probably the 911 operator. Both paid the house no mind.

Grossman, with the bomb in one hand, carried the body to the wild yard consumed by various weeds and neglected hedges that lined the wood fence separating the properties. He crossed a huge patch of old concrete cracked by the same weeds and brought the body to the hedges. Grossman dragged the body into a space between them and the fence. He doubted the police would search the yard. Not thoroughly enough anyway. All their attention should be on the front of the house since it appeared someone came in and smashed out the window from the inside.

Grossman jumped back and slapped his hand to his heart. Two people stood watching on the steps to the mudroom of the house. Two children dressed for the late 1800s. A boy and a girl no older than five. They stared at Grossman who shook his head at them. His heart calmed from the shock. Although he had never seen them before, he was aware of the extra residents. He had nothing to be afraid of but plenty to worry about at the moment.

Sweating, panting, and starving, Grossman exerted himself one last time in his damp suit to climb a fence and left the Radicci property. He found himself on Reservoir Avenue and walked back to his car on Booraem. Lorelei Collins, still on the phone, faced the house. By the time he drove off, the police arrived to investigate the break-in.

• • • •

The next day, Grossman and his employees, dressed as city sanitation workers, arrived at the Radicci house after Lorelei Collins and her daughter left for their daily Janet Moore Park visit. As his two employees stuffed Linderman's body into a thick black plastic trash bag and carried it out to their marked truck for disposal, Grossman snuck into the basement. All seemed well. Balanced. The Board should be satisfied for now.

When they left, Grossman returned to the GLM offices in Wayne where he made a few inquiries at Medical Center. He asked if he was able to visit Michelina Radicci. No, he was told. Michelina Radicci was not permitted any visitors besides immediate family. She was under police protection.

Police protection? Why?

The woman on the phone was not allowed to say. It didn't matter. Grossman was able to access a police report and read how someone tried to kill Michelina Radicci. That would explain why the sister was at her side all the time. But it didn't fully explain the blond woman on the motorcycle who planted the bomb or why the FBI agent was in the house.

It did explain that GLM and Grossman had nothing to do with it. In fact, he hoped that it escalated without harm to the house. He needed Michelina Radicci dead and if someone else wanted to take care of it, the better.

Girlfriend in a Coma

"Listen," Jody Coscarelli said. "I told the other agents all that I know."

"Of course, you did," Special Agent Linderman said a little too compliant. "As you should. But they want us to come out here to see if you remember anything more."

"Maybe something popped into your mind since the other agents were out here," Special Agent Shah said.

"Besides," Linderman said. "As far as we know, you never talked to the FBI. Only the ATF and local investigators. Correct?"

Jody shrugged and rubbed his tired eyes as he leaned against the threshold of his front door.

"I guess. I don't know. I hate to say this but you people all seem the same to me," Jody said. "Can you show me your badges and IDs again?"

Linderman smiled and pulled out his credentials. Shah, a woman from Pakistani parents with dark skin and long black hair pulled into a bun for the job, did the same. Jody leaned in and read the IDs.

"Yeah, okay," Jody said. "Come on in."

The agents entered the house on Booraem Avenue. It was a block away from Michelina Radicci's house. Not as old as hers but still part of the ancient history of the city. A two-level built in the 1930s with a small porch, a rust-covered awning, and a well-manicured flower garden Jody's mom enjoyed working on when she wasn't slaving shifts at Hackensack Hospital.

"You live alone?" Linderman asked, scanning around the front room.

"No," Jody said. "My mom lives here, too. She's at work. Do you need to talk to her?"

"How well does she know the suspect?"

"Miki? She used to come here all the time when we were kids but my mom hasn't spoken to her much since she moved to Manhattan."

"What about when Radicci returned from Manhattan?"

"My mom works the night shift. She sleeps during the day. They never ran into each other."

"Odd, since she's your girlfriend," Shah said, hanging by the door, her hands clasped in front of her lap, observing the two men standing around.

"Ex-girlfriend," Jody said. "I think. You two want to sit?"

Linderman sat on the offered couch. Shah remained where she stood by the door. Jody glanced at the woman who glared back with ice. Jody shrugged and sat in a chair across from the other agent. The coffee table littered with magazines, school books, notebooks, and a candy dish filled with mini chocolates divided them.

"You said, think," Linderman said, taking out his little notebook and pen. "What did you mean by that?"

Jody slacked his lanky body in the chair and grabbed the wooden arms. A bit of shame filled his stubbly face.

"We were having problems," he said. "But…I don't know. The last time we spoke it seemed like we might work them out."

"You wanted to work them out?"

"Of course."

"You love her, huh?"

"Yes. But not enough to help her kill an ATF agent."

"We're not here to accuse you of that," Linderman said. "We know that you were in an English Composition 2 class at NJCU when the crime happened. You're not a suspect."

"And I'm not a witness."

"But you were, are, in love with the suspect and we're hoping you can enlighten this investigation."

"Not going so well?" Jody asked.

Linderman squinted in annoyance and then glanced at his notes.

"How long were you and the suspect dating?"

"Until we broke up, a few months."

"That's not long. And you fell in love that quickly?"

"Miki and I grew up together," Jody said. "I was in love with her all my teens. You might say we picked up where we left off."

"Very sweet," Linderman said with a sour tone. "Why did you break up?"

"We had a fight?"

"Fight about what?"

"I don't see how it pertains to the crime or charges against her," Jody said, crossing his arms.

"We'll be the judges of that," Linderman said.

"That's what I'm worried about. You're not a judge. Nor are you someone in the position to judge her in opinion."

"So you were saying why you were dumped?" Linderman asked.

"I wasn't dumped."

"You dumped her?"

"No," Jody said, leaning forward, holding his spinning head in his hands. "We had a fight and...we couldn't resolve it."

"What did you fight about?"

"Sometimes, I don't even know anymore. It seemed stupid."

"At this point, everything is pertinent no matter how stupid it seems to a witness."

"I didn't witness the crime."

"You're a witness to the suspect," Linderman said. "You were saying about the break-up?"

"I thought she was cheating on me or something," Jody said, looking into Linderman's eyes, hoping his aggravation would scare the agent out of his house.

"What made you think that?"

"She disappeared for a few days."

"Disappeared? When?"

"It was in the winter."

Linderman frowned.

"We have no record of that from other witnesses," the agent said. "See, you just helped us out."

"I don't see how it helps you," Jody said. "She said she was on a tour for her work. Her artwork. The last one since she was retiring."

"She's twenty-one and retiring?" Linderman asked, shaking his head in wonder. "Am I in the wrong business."

"She was supposed to be gone for a few weeks but she returned early."

"Why did she cut the tour short?" Linderman asked.

"She didn't say."

"So that's what you fought about? She cut the tour short?"

"No," Jody said, throwing himself against the chair, slouching, spreading his sweat pant-covered legs. "She wasn't on a tour. She claimed to be in California. For some reason, it was a West Coast thing only. I was going to surprise her out there, have a romantic few days with her, but she was never there. Her publicist knew nothing about a final tour of her art."

"I would have been suspicious, too," Linderman said. "What did she have to say about it when you confronted her?"

"She said she couldn't say where she was and it was none of my business, I think."

"You think?"

"It happened so fast and so much was said. It was like an accident you see in the corner of your eye. You don't know exactly what happened but something bad happened."

"Interesting," Linderman said. "But you're sure she wasn't seeing another man. Or woman."

"She said she wasn't."

"So where do you think she was?"

"I don't know. Maybe her friends know."

"Her friends?"

"Yeah, I assume you spoke to them, too."

"We only spoke to her family. The only friends we know about are you and the man she was with, Michael Mallory."

"Oh," Jody said, yawning.

"We keeping you awake?" Linderman asked, all serious.

"I don't sleep well at night, lately."

"Guilty conscious can do that to a man."

Jody rolled his eyes.

"Give me the names of these friends," Linderman asked, his pen ready on the pad.

"Um, Gray and Miranda. They live in New York."

"Their last names?"

"I don't remember."

"You don't remember? She was your girlfriend and you don't remember her friends' last names?"

"I only met them once. Besides that, she rarely brought them up and, when she did, she only mentioned first names. That's all I know about them and that they were friends when she lived in New York. They seemed tight. Tighter than Miki and I at the time."

"Ms. Radicci sounds like a secretive woman. Must have been hard being her boyfriend. You can't have a stable relationship without trust. Clearly, she didn't trust you."

"Did you find out anything about the man she was with?" Jody asked, hiding the pain from Linderman's words.

"Michael Mallory? Not much. Recently, he moved to Jersey City from Bayonne. Before that, he lived in Freehold. The man is clean except for a few parking tickets that he promptly paid off," Linderman said. "You think they were together. Screwing or something?"

"No," Jody said. "She said she wasn't. I saw them together the morning of the...crime. She promised me he was only a friend."

"Did she say why they were together?"

"No. And she didn't tell me where she was going with him."

"You're either a confident man or a stupid man, Mr. Coscarelli."

"What do you mean?"

"If it were me, after what you've been telling us, I would be digging into her life with a snow CAT," Linderman said. "I have never encountered a more secretive and suspicious woman in my life."

• • • •

He should have gone home after class but the hospital's visiting hours were still open. He could sneak in at least thirty minutes with Miki's comatose body. Maybe get an update on her condition. A shot of hope that she's close to breaking out of the coma. Or, even better, she had awakened from the coma. What he would give to enter her room to find her smiling at him again.

Jody rushed off the bus on Grand Street in front of Jersey City Medical Center. His exhausted body lugged a backpack covered with buttons from local bands filled with the physics books for that day's class. Usually, he didn't mind having a class at 3:30 PM. It gave him time to catch up on his sleep. But lately, sleep eluded him. Much like good grades the last few months. Miki in her coma preoccupied his mind. He considered taking a semester off but his mother would probably talk him out of it. Miki nor his mother wouldn't want him to skip over his education for her health.

But what if she died while in the coma? He couldn't live with himself if that happened. Sure, he wasn't responsible for her. She made her choice to enter the house on St. Paul's and she suffered the consequences. By why? Why was she in there? Yeah, he knew about the story that guy Michael Mallory said to the agents. They heard a gunshot and they went to see if anyone needed help. But still, why were they even in the area? What was Miki doing all day with this Mallory?

The woman behind the front desk smiled at Jody and handed him his visitor badge. She asked if he knew where he was going.

"She's still in the same room on the third floor?" he asked.

The young Chicano woman who dressed as bright as her smile told him that she was there still.

With twenty minutes left, Jody went up to the third floor. As he walked/ran down the hall to Miki's room, he spotted the police officer standing next to the door. It had been a month since a cop stood guard. Why was he back?

The cop glared at Jody panting and sweating. Jody moved his brown bangs from his forehead and smiled.

"I'm visiting Michelina Radicci," he said.

"Are you immediate family?"

"Do I need to be?"

"Only immediate family can visit."

"Why?"

"I can't say."

"I don't understand," Jody said. "She was cleared as a suspect. You people couldn't find anything on her."

"You people?" the cop, the dark-skinned cop, asked.

Jody caught his open phrase and, embarrassed, said:

"I mean you police. She doesn't need to be protected anymore. Unless. Did something happen?"

"I can't say."

"Well, who can say? Is there someone I can talk to?"

"I don't know," the cop said. "I do know you need to calm down or I'm going to have to restrain you."

Realizing how close he was to the broad-chested cop who towered over him, he stepped back.

"I'm sorry," Jody said. "I'm frustrated. Listen, can I talk to someone inside? Is her mother in there? Veronica Radicci? She knows me. Please, can I speak to her?"

"Wait down the hall by the nurse's station," the cop said. "I'll go in and ask her. If she says No, then you leave. Got it?"

"Yes," Jody said. "Thank you. It's all I'm asking for."

Jody walked backward to the nursing station. The cop entered Miki's room. As close to alone as he could be, he shook his tense arms and rolled his head on his shoulders. He only had ten minutes to spend with Miki before the hospital kicked him out. If he could get in there.

"Jody?"

Veronica Radicci walked over. Behind her, the cop took his position at the door. Miki's mom appeared the same as the last time he saw her. Her round, pale face was pulled down with sorrow and worry. Her eyes still red from crying and her hair four days shy of a cleaning hung at her shoulders.

"Mrs. Radicci," he said, meeting her. "What the hell is going on? Is Miki okay?"

Veronica took Jody by the forearm, reminding him of an old lady even though she was far from that part of her life, and led him away from the nurses' station to the side of the elevator bank.

"Someone tried to kill, Miki," she whispered.

"What? Why?"

"We don't know. Prudy was there when it happened but she doesn't know who the woman was. She was wearing a mask."

"Maybe the woman from the house?" Jody asked. "Blake?"

"I don't know. But the police are protecting her in case it was her. Until they can figure it out."

"I can't believe this," Jody said. "I thought this was over. That all we had left was for Miki to wake up and... And things will go back to normal."

"I was thinking that, too," she said, smiling.

"Can I see her?"

"They won't let you in."

"Can you tell him I'm family? Maybe Miki and I are engaged?"

Veronica stared off to the side and tensed her lips into a grim line. Jody found it odd to suddenly break eye contact.

"We...someone else is posing as her fiance," she said. "We can't fit any more relatives."

"What do you mean?" Jody asked, appalled. "Who is posing as her fiance?"

"I have to get back. I'm sorry, Jody. You're a good boy and I love you like my own. I wish you could come inside but it's out of my hands."

Veronica offered her weak back and returned to the room. Jody wanted to scream at her, beg her to tell him what was going on but he knew the cop would only throw him out. Maybe arrest him and that would create more questions.

• • • •

Jody sat in a booth in the Monroe Diner across the street from Medical Center. Thankfully, the slightly barren four-lane Grand Street between him and the hospital didn't mess with his view of the front entrance. Sipping coffee and picking at cheese fries, he watched visitors and employees leave for the night. Some drove off in their cars parked in the lot, some waited for the bus, and some walked off. None of the

THE SENTINELS 79

faces appeared familiar. No faces from Miki's life that could pose as her fiance anyway.

His cell phone on the table vibrated a text alert. His mom was checking up on him, asking about how Miki was doing since she knew he was visiting her. Jody unlocked the phone and texted back:

She's the same. At the diner. Will be home soon.

Not that it mattered when he came home. His mom was working the night shift. Jody would only return to an empty house and a skull crowded with unanswerable questions.

"Hey, Jody," a man said behind him.

The slim guy with cropped red hair and pocked, pale skin slid into the booth across from him. He wore a yellow basketball jersey with the number 05 on it and black track pants. His hands rested on his lap under the table while his legs spread out as if he had the biggest pair of balls in the world.

"Gray, right?" Jody asked, tensing and leaning hard against the back of the booth.

"Yeah, man. You remember me!"

"We met at Miki's. The party. What are you doing here?"

"My girl is in the hospital," Gray said. "Why wouldn't I be here?"

"So you're posing as her fiance?"

Gray sputtered his lips and held back a loud laugh.

"No," he said. "Who would believe that?"

"They're only letting in immediate family. How are you sneaking in?"

Gray held up his black-gloved hands. He always wore them, from what Miki told Jody. Even during the hottest of summer days. Were they scarred? No. Miki left the question there for Jody to ponder.

"I'm her brother," Gray said. "And Miranda is her sister if you were wondering."

"You guys can't say I'm her brother, too?"

"Nah, man. We can't do that. That would be lying."

"What?" Jody said, feeling the room spin.

"Miki, Miranda, and I are like siblings," Gray said. "We been through deep shit together. Gray held up his right hand and wiggled the fingers. Jody noticed Gray was missing one, a pinkie. The sleeve the finger was supposed to be in was cut off and the hole was sewn shut. "I lost this finger helping out little sister a few years back."

"Putting up a shelf?" Jody ventured.

"Ha, no. I wish. It was back on Roosevelt Island. She never told you about it?"

"No," Jody sighed, tired. Tired of everything. "She never told me about how you lost your finger on Roosevelt Island."

"Fucked up story," Gray said. "A lot of it you won't believe. You had to be there to see it." Gray spaced out on his hand in front of him. Jody considered saying something to break him out of the trance. But then Gray said, "Bring it up to Miki when she wakes up. You can tell her I said it was okay. If she wants to talk about it. You should never force a woman to talk. Though, their mouths are raring to go most of the time. My wife talks a storm. I can barely keep up with her. Then later when we talk about something she gets mad at me because I didn't remember the previous conversation. In all honesty, I was spacing out. Her words are like music. They take me to another place, make my mind wander."

THE SENTINELS

"Gray, why are you here?" Jody asked.

"I'm watching out for my little sister," Gray said, lowering his hand back to his lap. "I told you that."

"No, why are you here with me?"

"You sound testy, yo."

"Can you blame me? The cops won't let me see Miki. Her mother won't help me see her. Then I find out you and this other woman are in and out of the room. Are you here to help me? Can you tell the cops or hospital that I'm her fiance?"

"That title is already taken," Gray said, shrugging.

"Who?"

"Mallory got it?"

"Michael Mallory?" Jody shouted. Realizing his volume, he then said in a lower level, "The guy from the house on St. Pauls?"

"That the man."

"Why the hell is he in there with her," Jody said. "For all we know he was the one responsible for bringing Miki into that house?"

"Really, dude?" Gray asked. "You really think Mallory, or anyone, can make Miki do something she doesn't want to do?"

"No, I guess not," Jody said. "But I don't understand what's going on."

"Someone wants Miki dead," Gray said, leaning in with his arms on the table. "You know that."

"Yeah," Jody said, leaning in, too. "Who?"

"We don't know. But we're taking it seriously."

"Who's we?"

"Her family."

Jody sighed and shook his head.

"Gray, I love Miki," he said. "I would do anything for her. If she's in trouble, I want to help. Why won't you bring me in?"

"From what I know, from what Prudy told me, you are not *in* yet," Gray said. "I know that sucks. I know that hurts. When my wife and I were separated she used to go out with other guys and involve my son sometimes and it hurt. I couldn't stand seeing them have fun with this other guy I didn't know and didn't want to know. I never felt so alone in my life."

"So what did you do?"

"I came to my senses and begged my wife to take me back where I belong."

"I was going to do that," Jody said. "We were going to meet that night. I was going to fix things."

"Awe, that's great. Miki loves you. She told me. You know, before. We all thought she was stupid for what she did. But, little sister had been burned before by guys. Especially guys who she opens her heart and secrets to."

"There's nothing that could scare me away from her," Jody said. "I accept her and love her no matter what."

Gray nodded, assured, and slipped out of the booth.

"Good to hear, man. I'll be seeing you."

"Wait," Jody said, turning out of the booth. "What about me helping?"

"You can't help," Gray said. "Not now. Maybe after Miki wakes up and you and her talk, you can help if she wants. But now, we have to respect her last actions. We have to keep it in the family. I promise you, we're taking good care of her. No one is going to get her."

Gray strutted out of the diner. Through the window, Jody watched him walk to the hospital parking lot. Grey entered

THE SENTINELS 83

a red two-door car that had seen better days, sitting in the driver's seat. Someone else was in the front passenger. Jody waited for the car to drive off. After all, visiting hours were over. But it remained in the lot. Probably all through the night after Jody finally went home.

• • • •

Jody skipped classes the next day. And the next. He spent all his time at Medical Center. During visiting hours, he sat in the lobby and watched the people move in and out while pretending to look at his phone or reading a newspaper or magazine left on the table. A few times he was dragged into a conversation by a lonely soul who wasn't even visiting. They had no place to go and liked to blend into the busy hospital lifestyle. Plus, they were kicked out of the Christ Hospital lobby for no reason.

When the lobby closed at 8 PM, Jody sat at the Monroe Diner. He drank cup after cup of coffee, mostly decaf, and ate cheese fries. The waitress who served him regularly, a woman in her late fifties with an exaggerated hourglass figure, started small-talking with him. Jody confessed he was visiting his girlfriend in a coma all day and he couldn't face being alone at home. Which wasn't far from the truth.

"Awe," the waitress said, tilting her head to one side and her hip to the other. "You're such a good boyfriend. I'm jealous of her."

Jody wasn't the only one watching the hospital. Gray's red car was there all day and night. So was the second passenger. A few times Gray left the car to wander around the hospital as if he were doing a security check. He also crossed to the diner to either use the bathroom or buy two cups of coffee to-go. Not once did he turn around to Jody. Not once did Jody call Gray over.

A wave of anger towards Gray grew inside Jody the last few days. Who the fuck was he that he got to see Miki? Did the cops really believe he was her brother? The cops would have checked it out, no? Maybe something sneaky was going on. No, something sneaky was definitely going on. Jody was tempted to run over to the car, pull Gray out, and demand answers.

Would he get them? Or would Gray and the other person beat the shit out of him?

Besides being a weakling who never won a fight, Jody couldn't risk it. Gray or someone else in the family could still approach him and need his help. Jody didn't want to ruin that moment. A moment of victory.

On the fourth night, leaving the closing lobby, Jody noticed one person in the red car. Only the driver. Curious, he steered closer for a better view. Only a few cars away from it, he made out a woman in her early twenties. A pleasant and familiar face with long straight, light brown hair. The street lights reflected against the gold crucifix around her neck. Miranda, one of Miki's family. He remembered her from the party.

Miranda glanced up from her lap and connected with Jody's eyes. For a second she appeared like a deer in headlights, then discomfort and confusion filled her face. Looking as if caught in a lie, she reluctantly waved to Jody. Instinctively, stupidly, he waved back.

In his usual booth at the diner, as he munched on cheese fries, Jody waited for Gray to enter the car. He would enter the car, right? He had been in it since Jody started his stalking routine. If not, then why the change tonight?

Around 10 PM, an ambulance entered the lot and stopped next to the red car. Jody squinted his eyes and wished he had brought binoculars with him but then he would be totally suspicious to the diner patrons and staff if he used them. It seemed like the ambulance driver and Miranda were talking.

A moment later, the ambulance approached the ER side of the hospital and backed its rear up into it. Miranda started the car and hovered close. Jody dropped cash on the table for his bill and rushed out of the diner.

He crossed the barren Grand Street and stopped close enough to see what was going on with the ambulance. The driver finally came out. Gray was dressed as an EMT. He opened the back doors. From the ER, an orderly pushed out a body with black hair wrapped in a blanket and hooked up to IV tubes, and loaded it into the ambulance as the cop observed. Prudy climbed inside.

It had to be Miki!

Michael Mallory who was also at her side, followed in. Gray closed the doors and returned behind the wheel.

An older woman with short hair who was with them swiftly walked to the red car. Miranda moved into the passenger side while the woman slipped behind the wheel.

The ambulance drove off and the red car followed. Jody, never so helpless in his life, chased after it until his legs gave out and his lungs burned, which wasn't very far. They were gone. Maybe to the Turnpike, maybe deeper into Jersey City, or maybe into New York.

Miki was gone.

"Fuck," Jody screamed, blending in with the rest of the Jersey City's dead nightlife.

He turned back to the diner, to the bus stop, with no other choice but to go home. Jody's self-pity made the world oblivious. He didn't even notice the blond woman wearing a black helmet on a sleek motorcycle heading in the same direction as the ambulance.

Definite Doors

Veronica Radicci usually visited her daughter in the late morning before she started her late shift at the Miss America Diner. For the last few months, she took the bus to Jersey City Medical Center from West Side Ave then, afterward, back to West Side where she walked a few blocks to work. A few times she was late for her shift. Not because she couldn't leave her daughter's side, though it was hard to do, but due to the crappy transit system.

Her boss Caruthers gave her shit once and a while for being late. Veronica reminded him she asked for an early shift so she could visit her daughter at night.

"You know," Veronica stressed. "My daughter who has been in a coma."

He knew. Maybe he didn't care. Maybe because Miki was suspected of killing the ATF agent that day in the exploding house, he thought Veronica wasn't worth the effort. Maybe he didn't give a shit about a killer. He never said it to Veronica's face. He always repeated how he difficult it was to maneuver the schedule. None of the other girls wanted to switch. Girls. Like all the waitresses were under eighteen. Most of them were close to Veronica's age floating around forty to sixty.

Caruthers never punished her for being late. He never demanded that she make up the fifteen or thirty minutes like with the other 'girls'. Maybe he was being compassionate. Maybe if and when Miki woke from her coma, he would be a bastard again.

By now, all the nurses and hospital staff recognized Veronica. They waved or said hello. She was the mother of their only coma patient. Usually the hospital and insurance company transferred someone like Miki to another center or released her to be treated by a visiting nurse at home but someone was paying the bill. Not the insurance company and definitely not Veronica who couldn't afford the high price of daily care even for herself.

Not that she wouldn't do it if she could. Veronica would do anything for her daughter. She managed Miki's art career when she was a child. A career that went well until money disappeared. Miki blamed Veronica and Michael, her ex-husband. Veronica tried to tell Miki who was fifteen years old back then she had nothing to do with it. Miki wouldn't listen. Her anger and betrayal made her deaf.

Soon after, Miki emancipated herself and moved out of Jersey City to New York where she bought a condo and continued her art career. She lived with her grandfather Blaise Radicci, Michael's father, who drove a bus for the city. That was reassuring. Someone of her blood was watching out for her. Until Blaise disappeared almost four years ago with Michael's brother Anthony who escaped from federal prison at the same time.

Veronica followed her daughter's career through the art trades and continued to be proud of her success. She was not proud of the gossip. The media sometimes branded her a wild teen clubbing around the city where she got drunk and slept with celebrities. Maybe some of it was true. She hoped not. She prayed not. In the end, there was nothing she could do without suffering the charges of grand theft and a lawsuit.

THE SENTINELS

Unknowingly, Miki moved back to Jersey City last year and popped back into her life. She bought Veronica's old house she never liked but Michael was fascinated with at first. Then the creepy nights and architecture started to bother him as much as her. A few times it felt like someone was walking through the house. Watching them.

They couldn't get rid of the house at the time. The housing market sucked. Without the management salary from her daughter and having to go back to shitty jobs like retail and waitressing, they fell behind on the high mortgage payments.

No, Michael Radicci couldn't financially help out. Since he had been to prison a few times, the job market ignored him. Although he never talked about it, Veronica knew Michael was doing odd illegal jobs to make money. Probably hijacking trucks and selling the merchandise again. Something Blaise Radicci used to do before he fell in love with Carmella, Veronica's mother-in-law, and joined the army.

God. This family.

Sometimes, Veronica wished she never fell in love with Michael Radicci and his beautiful smile and attractive soul and logical levelheadedness. Sometimes, she wished he was with her now. Now, at their daughter's side. But he was nowhere to be found. He might even be dead.

Veronica entered the private hospital room and found her daughter still in a coma. Every day, disappointment welcomed her. She wished Miki would open her eyes and smile at her when she entered. Miki would smile, right? The last time they talked, they were on sort of good terms. If Miki didn't smile, Veronica would be fine, too. As long as she was awake and healthy.

Then Veronica would shovel in the guilt. What was she doing at that house on St. Pauls? Why did she go in there? Why was she even walking around with that guy Michael Mallory who Veronica never met before? And most importantly, what the hell had been going on in her life since she retired from the art world?

Miki's life was filled with secrets. Not too many lies. More like a refusal to answer because any word about a subject would be a thread for Veronica to pull and reveal the truth.

"Oh, my sweet, girl," Veronica said, sitting beside her and holding her cool pale hand with the IV in it. "Why is the truth so hard? Do I make it that difficult for you to confide in me?"

The door opened and a light-skinned teenager wearing a *Hello, Kitty* t-shirt that matched her *Hello, Kitty* canvas sneakers and a pair of biker shorts entered. As usual, the girl avoided Veronica's eyes and sat in the chair on the other side of Miki. The girl wasn't ignoring Veronica. Although, she would understand if she did. Veronica wasn't too nice to Miki's half-sister when she first met her. She was Michael Radicci's illegitimate child. Michael conceived her in prison. A possibility that brought up more questions. What the hell was going on in that prison?

"Hello, Prudy," Veronica said. "What are you doing here today? Don't you have school?"

Prudy waved and shook her head, making her pinched-out curly hair that could use a wash shiver. Veronica realized it was Saturday. Of course, Prudy would be here at her sister's side on the weekend. The girls loved each other. She had never seen two siblings so attached at the hip. No, she had. Michael and Anthony Radicci were close. Dangerously close when their crimes were concerned. Could the girls be involved with their father's business? Was that why Miki was in that house?

Exhaustion pressed down on Veronica. She released Miki's hand and leaned back in the seat. She worked seven days a week to afford the basics she needed to live. Eight, sometimes twelve, hours a day. She had been doing this for years and it had been straining her brain to the point where every day was the same. There was never a distinction. And why was she working like this? She gained no pleasure from it. No breaks.

Veronica should quit. She should be at her daughter's side every day and all day. But then she would lose her apartment, fall deeper into debt, and be on the street. Well, she would be in Miki's mysteriously paid hospital room until she woke up. Then she would have to find a new place to crash.

• • • •

One day in late June, Veronica Radicci escaped the humid press of air to find salvation in the hospital. They were blasting the air-conditioning, thankfully. But when she arrived on the third floor and found a uniformed cop and two men in suits talking, a pain wrapped around her heart and sweat broke out all over her body.

"What happened to my daughter?" Veronica demanded before she even reached five feet away from the group of men.

George Dunderman, one of the suits, turned to her. Veronica knew him as head of hospital security when Miki was first admitted. They weren't sure if that psycho Blake girl was going to come after her since Miki survived the house explosion. Dunderman explained the procedures designed with the cops to keep Miki safe. The other man she didn't recognize but since he had a badge and a gun attached to his waist she assumed he was a detective.

"Mrs. Radicci," Dunderman said. "We've been trying to contact you."

Veronica didn't remember her cell ringing on her way up here but she always kept her phone buried in her bag and on vibrate so it was possible she missed the calls.

"Is Miki all right?" she asked, pushing the heavy door open.

The detective blocked her way without touching her. Veronica seemed like a live wire which was understandable at the moment.

"Your daughter is fine," he said. "As you can see."

Yes, Miki was still on the bed and hooked up to machines. A few others were in the room dusting for prints and vacuuming for fibers. Relief teased Veronica but refused to flood her.

"What happened?"

Someone tried to kill Miki last night. A woman with a gun. The woman might have been successful if Prudy hadn't walked in and interrupted her.

"Is Prudy okay?" she asked, grabbing Dunderman's arm through the blurry swirl around her.

Prudy's fine. She's in the cafeteria eating breakfast with one of the guards.

Was this woman Aurora Blake, the detective didn't know. Based on video cameras and witnesses, the woman wore a visored cap and a black cotton mask over her mouth and nose. She was never at the front desk for a visitor pass.

"And no one thought she was suspicious, her wearing a mask?" Veronica asked, appalled.

Not in a hospital where visitors do not want to catch any germs consonantly floating in the air.

Fine.

Okay.

Veronica accepted that. But still.

Someone tried to kill her daughter.

Again.

"Can I see her?" she asked.

"Soon," the detective said. "The techs should be done soon."

Veronica wandered to the bench by the nurses' station. Her butt slammed down and her face fell into her hands. Miki, Miki, she thought. What has been going on in your life that people want you dead?

Someone tapped her shoulder.

Veronica looked up into Prudy's unemotional face staring off down the hall. The face of her husband's illegitimate child. A face that shared the lower part of his features. The product of his love for another woman. Veronica didn't care. She jumped up and hugged Prudy.

"Thank...thank you," she wept.

The teen squirmed out of her arms and stepped back, shaking her head.

Veronica remembered. Miki told her once. Prudy was autistic. She didn't like to be touched. Rarely by friends and definitely by strangers.

"I'm sorry," Veronica said. "I forgot."

Prudy crossed her arms and nodded.

For now on, Veronica would work at becoming the friend of the young woman who saved her daughter's life.

• • • •

"Time off?" Caruthers said. "Are you nuts?"

Veronica, dressed for work in her powder pink uniform and standing behind the counter with him, crossed her arms and rolled her eyes.

"Did you hear what I said?" she asked. "I need time off. I need to be with my daughter for a while."

"Your daughter in a coma? Are they not taking care of her?"

"It's not that." Veronica bit her lip. No way she was going to tell him about how someone tried to kill Miki. The police and the hospital promised to keep it out of the press and, so far in the last 48-hours, it had been. "I need to be by her side."

Caruthers also crossed his arms, sighed hard, and leaned against the counter as if his stumpy legs were about to give out.

"How long?" he asked, squinting.

"I don't know. Until she wakes up or… I don't know."

"Until she wakes up? Jesus Christ. I can't shuffle the schedule around that long. Some of these girls will not have it. Some of them have kids." Veronica knew none of them had kids. At least, kids under eighteen they had to rush home to care for. "You do know that I'm not only responsible for this business but for the lives of all the people who work here?"

"I don't understand why you're giving me a hard time," Veronica said, shifting her hands to her hips and raising her voice. What few people in the diner that early afternoon turned their attention to them. "The college barely has activity in the summer. You're only going to serve the deadbeat regulars until September."

"Don't remind me," he said.

"Yeah, well, there you go. Me taking a few weeks off for medical reasons shouldn't be a problem."

"So now it's a few weeks?" He glared with suspicion. "Before you didn't know how long."

"Can you do this for me or not?" she asked.

"Let me think about it."

Veronica slammed her fist on the counter, wishing it was his face.

"Forget it," she said, removing the apron over her uniform. "You don't have to worry about it. I quit."

If someone didn't give them their attention, they were giving it now.

"Quit!" he said, chasing after Veronica as she moved out from behind the counter. "That's even worse!"

"Not my problem," Veronica said, ignoring the eyes of the amazed and entertained patrons and staff. "If you can't help me out in my time of need, if you can't do this one thing for me after all the years and hours I slaved for you, then it's not my problem."

"Yeah, well it's going to be your problem when that psycho killer daughter of yours wakes up and you come crying back for your job," Caruthers said.

Veronica stopped at the front door, whipped around, and plowed her fist into his jaw. Caruthers, stunned, stumbled back. Veronica took the chance and kicked him in the nuts with her soft-soled white sneakers. The portly man folded over as his face turned tomato red and nausea crawled up his throat.

"Fuck you," Veronica said.

She left the diner and the laughing and cheering patrons and staff behind.

• • • •

Prudy, munching on a snack-sized bag of crunchie cheese doodles, glanced up at Veronica entering the room. Miki's mother dropped her bag as if filled with rocks on the floor and kissed her daughter's dry forehead.

"I'm back, baby girl," she whispered. "I'll be around more often now."

Veronica sat on the chair and took Miki's hand. Prudy munched and spaced out.

"Are you curious about why I'm back already?" she asked the teen.

Prudy nodded and chewed, her attention on the little bag.

"I quit my job. The son of a bitch wouldn't give me time off. You believe that shit?" Prudy snickered. Veronica smiled back. "Well, maybe he would have done it if I didn't punch him in the face and kick him in the balls."

Prudy stopped chewing and almost looked Veronica in the eye. Her brows went up in question, then she snorted in laughter.

"It's funny. I want to laugh," Veronica said. "But now I need another job. I might have enough in my savings for a few month's rent. Not like I have a reason to go home."

Prudy placed the bag on the bed and pulled out her notepad and pen. She wrote:

You can stay with us if you have to.

Veronica closed her eyes as a deep swelling sensation bloomed around her heart and urged the tears to flow.

"Even though I was so terrible to you since I met you?" Veronica asked.

Prudy nodded.

"Thank you," she croaked.

• • • •

That night, a nurse checking Miki's machines and bags woke Veronica up with her movements. The nurse apologized to Veronica.

"No, it's okay," she said, straightening in the chair. "Didn't even know I conked out."

When the nurse left, Veronica took Miki's hand again and noticed Prudy sitting with her eyes closed. Her body was too tense to be asleep. Was she meditating? Veronica kept quiet and studied their faces. Despite the difference in skin tone, she noticed how the sisters shared their father's wide nose and strong chin.

Veronica smiled. Michael would have loved that about the girls. He loved heredity. The way parts of people live on through DNA. If biology was different, Veronica would have had a second child with him. Soon after Miki was born, Veronica wanted to do an endometrial ablation to end her unbearable menstrual cycles. The doctor found a cyst on her ovary. It was cancerous. To play it safe, they removed her uterus. That was the end of the cancer and the end of her baby-making days.

Prudy opened her eyes and glanced around.

"Sleeping?" Veronica asked.

Shaking her head, she grabbed her water bottle off the floating table and sipped it.

"I was thinking how you and Miki look a lot like your father," Veronica said.

Prudy eased the bottle back on the table.

"Have you seen a picture of him?" she asked.

Prudy nodded.

"Have you ever met him?"

Prudy shook her head.

"That's terrible," she said. "A girl needs her father in her life. He sets the standard for the kind of man she picks to be her partner."

Prudy smirked.

"Well, I always thought so. Times are different now. You girls live in different times."

Silence filled the room. Squeaky shoes and wheels snuck in through the ajar door to the hall.

"Did your father pass on anything to you?" Veronica asked.

Prudy blank-stared at the bed.

"You know, like Miki. An ability to feel what other people feel?"

Prudy nodded and shook her head. She wrote on her pad and passed it to Veronica.

Write your cell number down.

"Um, okay," she said. Maybe the girl wants to text her answers.

After using Prudy's pen, she passed the pad back. The teen glanced at it and closed her eyes. Veronica's cell vibrated with an incoming call. The number 222-222-2222 came up as unidentified. Prudy stabbed her finger at the phone.

Veronica, unsure, answered it.

"This is part of my ability," a sexless computer voice said from the phone.

Veronica's mouth dropped as she studied the teen sitting still with her eyes closed.

"This is you?"

"Yes."

"Prudy?"

"Duh."

"Oh, my God," Veronica said.

"God has nothing to do with it," Prudy said. "But heredity definitely does."

Veronica smiled. For the first time in a long time, she felt like someone had finally escorted her through a long closed door.

• • • •

Veronica had no idea who this woman in her sixties with short blond and white hair was entering her daughter's secure room but she sensed she knew all about her. She certainly knew Prudy who waved to the woman.

"Who are you?" Veronica asked.

"For now, I'm Miki's grandmother." The woman sat in a chair against the wall, under the bolted television whispering local news. "And you're Veronica Radicci."

Veronica glanced at the closed door behind her as if maybe the cop outside was with them and could clear out the insanity that entered the room.

"Funny," Veronica said. "You don't look like my mother."

The woman pulled out a small box of animal crackers. She offered the open box to Prudy who took one and then to

Veronica who ignored it. Unwounded by the refusal, the woman snacked.

"I'm posing as Michael's mother," she said. "Carmella."

"Carmella has been dead for almost twelve years," Veronica spat, trying to keep her rage in check. Who did this woman think she was posing as Carmella Radicci who helped her so much when Miki was little? "And I don't think this is funny."

"I wasn't trying to be funny," the woman said. "I was trying to be honest. I figured, since I knew Carmella well, I should pose as her for the cops." She pointed to the visitor pass on the breast of her denim jacket. The name read Carmella Radicci. "Normally I would pose as myself, but this is a difficult situation."

"Who the fuck are you?" Veronica asked, her voice rising.

"Shh," the woman said. "You don't want the cop to come in here."

"He'll throw you out as soon as I tell him the truth."

"No one is going to throw anyone out." The box of animal crackers left the woman's hand and floated to a few inches from Veronica's face. The mother deflated, not at all bothered by the bit of telekinesis. "Get that shit out of my face."

The box returned to the woman's hand.

"I know," she said. "I eat too many of these things. I should cut down. But I do enjoy their aftertaste and I go to the gym three times a week to burn them off."

"Okay," Veronica said. "You're one of…those people. So what's your real name."

"Ruby Stahl."

Veronica thought for a moment and shook her head.

"I don't think Carmella ever mentioned you."

"She shouldn't," Ruby Stahl said. "Before she got married we used to work together. After that, we rarely saw each other. She promised she wasn't going to have anything more to do with...the business."

"So why are you here now? I assume you and Miki know each other."

"Miki and I work together."

"What do you mean, work?"

"I can't say. Miki can tell you if she wants, but I'm not at liberty. Though I should be able to trust you considering you know a lot about the family's abilities, I'm going to leave the trust to Miki."

Veronica sighed and rubbed her eyes.

"You know what she's talking about?" Veronica asked Prudy on the other side of the bed. Prudy nodded. "Figures."

"Don't be so frustrated," Stahl said. "I'm here to help. We're here to help. Soon I should be able to have someone with my ability to sit with Miki. He'll protect her better than the cop outside."

"Let me guess," Veronica said. "He'll pose as Miki's brother."

"No, that title is already claimed by Gray. This man will be Miki's fiance. Don't worry. They know each other already. Only people who know Miki and Miki knows are involved."

"Great," Veronica said, filled with sarcasm. "Do you know who tried to kill my daughter?"

"No. Maybe. Based on the hospital footage and our sources, we don't know for sure," Stahl said. "I am positive it was not Aurora Blake, the woman who almost killed Miki in the house explosion. We suspect she's out of the state by now."

"Why would someone want my daughter dead?"

Stahl shrugged and focused on a pinched elephant.

"I don't know."

"You don't seem surprised that someone wants to kill her," Veronica said.

"In our line of work, you pick up an enemy or two that gains the privilege of life," Stahl said. "Or, it could be someone we don't know about. Maybe someone picked out Miki and decided she needed to be dead."

"This is insane," Veronica said, her voice rising. "What the hell is my daughter involved in?"

"I can't say."

"Do you know?" she asked Prudy.

The teen grabbed the arms of the chair and shook her right knee from side to side.

"Well, it seems like Miki is well-protected," Veronica said. "Maybe I should leave."

"No, you should stay. A girl needs her mother," Stahl said, rising. "Though I never met my mother. I was abandoned. I found a mother in others. Those women are as important. I have some preparations to make."

"Preparations for what?" Veronica asked.

"You'll see when I confirm them."

"You mean you'll keep me in the loop?"

"Maybe outside the loop but very close to it."

Stahl pocketed her animal crackers and left the room.

Veronica slammed back in the chair and shook her fists in frustration.

"I don't like that woman," she said. "I don't like what's going on."

THE SENTINELS 103

Prudy stared off and held her sister's hand which infuriated Veronica even more.

• • • •

More visitors came into the room over the next few days. Miki's brother and sister. Or, as Veronica knew them, Gray Delisle and Miranda Cohn. She also knew of their psychic abilities. She had met them before at Miki's house. Veronica was glad to see them and exchanged hugs with them. Finally, familiar faces with answers.

Veronica was wrong. Gray and Miranda had no answers to her questions about what was going on with this mysterious Ruby Stahl. Maybe they were never told. But they assured her no one was going to hurt Miki. They were prepared to give their lives for her. Veronica believed them. She trusted them.

The third visitor, she was anxiously expecting. Miki's fiance. She knew him. Not personally but through the news stories a few months ago. Michael Mallory. The man who almost died with Miki in the house. He walked with a cane and was seriously overweight. This was the man who was going to protect Miki?

"From your expression, you don't think I'm worthy or much to protect your daughter," Mallory said, sitting in the chair under the television. "But I'm quite spry and fast on my feet."

Prudy sputtered a laugh. Mallory smiled at the teen. Veronica rolled her eyes.

"I assume you have something to do with Ruby Stahl," Veronica said. "You have an ability, too."

"I do," Mallory said. "Telekinesis."

"But you and Miki almost got killed," Veronica said, leaning forward in her chair, her elbows on her knees. "Weren't you supposed to protect her then?"

He closed his eyes a moment. Perhaps finding the right words for her question. His lower lip pressed into his upper.

"That was a big cluster fuck and Ruby blames herself," Mallory said. "Miki and I were trapped with someone few people experienced. Stahl doesn't think Blake is involved. So, I believe I can handle anything that comes into this room."

"Excuse me if I'm not assured," Veronica said.

• • • •

Assure or not, Veronica had no choice.

Especially, two nights later.

At 9:36 PM, the cop led in Ruby Stahl and an orderly.

"What's this?" Veronica, her brain waking from the fog of being in a doze, asked. "What's going on?"

"Ms. Radicci is being transferred," the orderly said.

"What?" Veronica rubbed her sleep-crusted eyes and looked at Prudy who was wide awake on the other side of the bed. "Did you know about this?"

Prudy stood and nodded. Mallory, at the foot of the bed, also stood from his chair and avoided her eyes.

"Can you give us a minute before you prepare her?" Stahl said to the cop.

When the cop and the orderly left, Stahl approached Veronica.

"We're moving her someplace safe until she wakes up," she said.

"You're telling me now? How long have you known?"

"Not long."

Veronica moved her bag from the floor to the chair and gathered her cell phone and other items that found their way out during her last few days of living in the room.

"I'm her mother," she said, expressing her annoyance by throwing the items into the bag without care. "You should have told me."

"I saw no reason to give you much information since you're not coming with us," Stahl said. "Plus, the fewer people who know the better."

Veronica stopped and glared at Stahl.

"She's my daughter," she stated. "What are you trying to tell me?"

"We only have room for a few," Stahl said. "Recently, someone tried to break into Miki's house while her friend and daughter were sleeping there. It's not safe for Prudy now. She will come with her. And, of course, Michael here will be joining."

"Why do I get the sense that this is not legal?" Veronica asked.

"It's legal on paper and for anyone to look into," Stahl said. "Between us, it is something different." She placed her hand on Veronica's forearm. "I promise, Miki will be safe where she's going. It's not only me who is a part of this. There are others. Others like her."

Wringing her hands, Veronica glanced at Mallory. He nodded, his expression sincere. Prudy offered nothing. When she looked upon Miki, the tears flowed with the sob.

"Will I see her again?" she asked.

"When she wakes up," Stahl said.

"What if she doesn't wake up?" Veronica asked.

The room fell silent.

Not receiving an answer, Veronica sat back down and took her daughter's limp, pale hand. She stared at her tranquil face. Veronica saw the baby inside her grown daughter's features. The little baby that came out of her belly who she promised to protect no matter what happened in life. The baby she would die for. The baby she promised to be there for when her baby couldn't be there for herself.

Her baby was a woman with her own life. A life she didn't know much about. A life resulted in someone wanting to kill her. A life filled with friends who shared her ability. Something Veronica couldn't do. Something her father definitely could do. Miki needed these people. Her people. Her other family. Veronica had faith in their love for her daughter. If she didn't, she would go insane with worry and regret.

Veronica leaned in, kissed her daughter's face, and promised they would see each other again.

"You just better wake up," she whispered in Miki's ear, squeezing her hand. "Or, I'll make you wish you stayed where ever you are."

She giggled through her tears, kissed her again, and then straightened. Her eyes on Miki, Veronica said:

"She can go now."

Night Running

"You okay?" Miranda Cohn sitting at her side asked.

Ruby Stahl's eyes struggled to stay awake while driving Gray's car down the New Jersey Turnpike. If she crashed it, the damage would be an improvement to the exterior. Thankfully, not many cars were on the road tonight and she would only crash into a gully.

"The engine is fine as wine," Gray told her a few days ago. "You don't need to worry about the sweet shell."

He was correct. The little red Ford built fifteen years ago had a pristine engine under its dented hood and was able to keep up with the ambulance ahead of it. Still, she should have brought a giant cup of coffee with her before they started their trip.

"I'm fine," Stahl said. "How are you?"

"Oh," the woman in her early twenties with the cleanest long, light brown hair and clearest complexion Stahl had ever seen sighed. Miranda fingered the tiny gold crucifix resting on the breast of her often conservative dress with floral prints. "I could be better. I could be home praying for Miki."

"What you're doing now is better than prayers," Stahl said. "But if you want to pray now, I won't mind. It's a long trip and it might keep me awake."

"A trip to where, though?"

Stahl forced her eyes open, focusing on the fake license plate on the back of the ambulance. She tested how long it would take not to blink. Maybe she should eat some animal crackers instead.

"I know we're going to the Colony but where is this colony?" Miranda asked.

"South."

"Carolina?"

"One of them."

"Guess all answers will be revealed when we get there."

Miranda yawned. Stahl did the same and threw the young woman a dirty expression.

"Don't do that," she said. "I hope you don't do that the whole drive down."

"Yawn?"

"It's going to make me tired. If you need to, you can sleep in the back."

Miranda glanced into the rear seat.

"As tempting as it is, I'll stay up here and help you stay awake," she said, jovially, her slight southern accent sounding stronger.

"Not with that yawning."

"Sorry," Miranda said.

Stahl considered switching the wheel with Miranda. Clearly, she had more sleep than her the last few days. The woman in her late mid-sixties snuck catnaps the last few days making arrangements for Miki Radicci's illegal transfer out of the hospital. Her stomach was so nervous the whole time she wasn't able to eat. Not even her favorite animal crackers.

Movement in the rearview mirror caught her eye. A motorcycle with its lights off sped up on them. It then swung up her side into the second lane and kept pace with her. Blond hair whipped out from the black helmet.

"Who's this?" Miranda said.

"Trouble."

"No," she said, looking out her window. "I mean this."

Another biker paced them on the shoulder. This one had no hair sticking out but the contours of the body in black clothing were definitely male compared to the curves of the one on her left.

"More trouble," Stahl said, now more alert with adrenalin pumping through her brain.

The bikers reached into their black leather jackets, pulled out automatic handguns, and aimed them at Stahl and Miranda.

• • • •

Prudy Radicci closed her eyes and entered the ether. She was curious about what happened to her favorite FBI agent Raymond Resnick after her little scam on his computer. Based on the Bureau's website, he was no longer listed in the directory of agents. Did they fire him or suspend him during an investigation? Prudy imagined they suspended him. After all, he was blackmailed (not a really since the BitCoin address she gave was fake) and someone else sent out the fake video of him masturbating to porn on his computer.

No, Resnick should be fine in time. Stuck in an embarrassing hell but fine.

Prudy only wished she could have signed her real name to the blackmail email. That she could have told him it was her and he shouldn't mess with her again. Maybe he was smart enough to know it was her. In time.

Now, what to do about Jordan?

She couldn't play the same kind of scam with her. Not after what she went through last year. Prudy had to be creative in a way that would cause little lasting damage to her ex-girlfriend's brain.

Or did she even need to bother doing anything to Jordan? She had to be suffering enough for what she tried to pull on Prudy. God! The rage still flowed strongly in her.

Jordan tried to explain through texting and emailing. No way she would be brave enough to show her face. She wrote to Prudy about how Resnick hinted he would tell Jordan's mom about her and Prudy's relationship. But Prudy wasn't having it. She didn't care if Jordan's mom knew about her daughter's sexuality. Prudy was sick of sneaking around. Maybe Jordan screwing up Resnick's plan was a good thing. Maybe he told Jordan's mom about their relationship.

She hoped so.

But would it matter now?

Would Prudy ever take Jordan back after such a betrayal?

Prudy, sitting on the bench built into the length of the ambulance, opened her eyes. Miki lay on the stretcher. IV tubes fed into the top of her hand and a heart monitor softly beeped on the shelf above her head. Her sister's face seemed so calm. Something she rarely saw since they met almost five years ago.

"You ever been to this place?" Michael Mallory asked, sitting on the other side of the bench and close to the rear double doors. "This Chatham Colony?"

Prudy, eyes on her sister, shook her head and tapped her right hand fingers on her thigh.

"Me neither," Mallory said. "First I ever heard about it but I haven't known Ruby too long. I thought because you two had a longer history."

Prudy shook her head. She considered calling his cell number if he had one on him, but her brain was too tired to jump into the ether again tonight. Also, cell phones were not permitted tonight. Someone could use them to track their location.

"I should have brought something to read," Mallory said. "Like a book or magazine. I usually read on my phone but..."

Only those in the Tenebrous knew of the Chatham Colony. It was the safest place in the world and occupied by psychics. No neurotypicals were allowed even though the colony was founded by two NTs. Mr. and Mrs. Cavendish were long dead and now it was one hundred percent psychic.

I was raised there, Stahl texted Prudy the other day. *And your grand uncle Enzo and his family lived there a long time. He was wanted by the police and a few psychos but they never found him.*

Enzo is the one who has the same ability as me, Prudy wrote back. *He can access the internet and computers with his brain. Is he still alive?*

I can't say, Stahl wrote. *But they never found him while he was there.*

Prudy tried to be reassured with such a cryptic answer. She would like to meet Enzo Noto if he was alive. He should be in his early seventies if he was still breathing. Or even one of his children or grandchildren. They had to have the same ability as Prudy, right?

"Yo, how's it going up there?" Mallory called to the front of the ambulance. His voice carried through the little open plexiglass window. Gray made an okay sign with his hand.

"Smooth as owl shit," he said. "If it stays like this, we should hit South Carolina by dawn."

"Nice," Mallory yawned.

Prudy took out her notepad and wrote

You were with my sister when she went away last winter?

"Yeah," Mallory said. "Where I met her. It was a training thing with Tenebrous. But it didn't turn out that way. Some psycho tried to kill us."

Is the psycho dead?

"I hope so," Mallory said. "But not by us. He got away."

You saved Miki's life.

"I saved a few lives. If you don't mind me being so bold."

I do not mind.

Mallory chuckled.

"Miki's a badass," Mallory said. "And a pain in the ass. I like her. I feel bad about what happened back in April at that house. I should have done something more but...I don't know."

Stop living in the past.

"Yeah, I know," he said. "I'm trying. I'm here now in the moment. Ruby said everything should go well. I probably won't use my ability at all. But just in case, if I do, I'm all on it. No one is going to harm your sister."

Not while you're alive.

"Shit. I don't plan on dying."

Prudy, staring at Miki, nodded. She then crossed her arms and rested her eyes.

A metal crack from outside.

Prudy broke out of a doze. Miki was fine. Her machine was beeping.

"What the hell was that?" Gray shouted from the driver's seat.

Mallory peeked out the small rear window.

"No fucking way, man," he whispered.

. . . .

"Ruby!" Miranda screamed, grabbing onto the older woman's arm and staring hard at the man with the gun aimed at her head.

"I know," Stahl shouted.

The cyclist on the left fired at Stahl.

She stomped the brake.

The bullet shot through the empty air and almost hit the motorcycle on the shoulder. Both machines swerved into the right lane, almost colliding, and between the red car and the ambulance.

"Who are they?" Miranda asked, grabbing the dashboard, her eyes wide with fright.

"I don't recognize them right now," Stahl said. "But I'll be sure to ask them later." With her head, she motioned to the backseat. "Go into my bag and hand me my gun."

Miranda pulled the bag from the back floor to her lap and rummaged inside it.

"Where is it?" she asked, exasperated.

Stahl stomped the gas and tested to see if the pick-up in the car was as Gray bragged. With a sudden jolt of force, her body pressed to the seat. Miranda screamed and grabbed the dash.

The car closed in on the two motorcycles, urging them closer to the back of the ambulance.

"Oh, my God," Miranda said. "You're going to kill them if you get any closer."

"I'm hoping they know that, too."

From the angle in the driver's seat, it was tough to see how close she was to their rear tires. Stahl would have to be satisfied by seeing their bodies fly through the air or under the car.

"Ruby!" Miranda screamed again, now pressing her sneakered feet to the dash.

The motorcycles split into the other lanes, almost hitting Stahl. She took her foot off the gas. The red car nearly rammed the back of the ambulance. Space grew between the two vehicles. The motorcycles were behind them now.

Stahl smiled at Miranda and was about to say something witty when she realized the young woman was cuddling her gun. The gun innocently pointed at Stahl.

"Mind if I have that now so you don't kill me," she asked.

"I hate guns," Miranda said, passing it, holding it with two pinched fingers by the handle.

With her right hand, Stahl gripped the automatic. Then, holding the wheel with it, she pressed the button on the door with her left to lower the window. The humid night air whipped into the car and filled their ears with a harsh howl. Stahl aimed the gun out the window and to the rear, her head following.

"What are you doing?" Miranda panicked.

"Grab the wheel."

"Are you serious?"

Not waiting for an answer, Miranda gripped the wheel to keep the car straight. Stahl aimed at the blond. She had a clear shot if it wasn't for that pedestrian driver in the BMW a few cars back.

The blond brought out her gun from her leather jacket again and fired at the Ford.

Stahl slipped back in, having no idea where that bullet went but glad it didn't enter her body.

"Shit," she said, taking the wheel from Miranda.

Another shot from the biker. The rear window shattered into a spiderweb.

"Down," shouted Stahl.

Miranda hid behind the seat, pressing to the floor and covering her head with her arms.

The two bikers sped up and resumed their previous places. The blond covered the second lane and the other raced up the shoulder to position between the Ford and the ambulance which was a good quarter mile ahead.

"Going to try it again, huh," Stahl muttered, spotting the blond aiming a gun at her. "So will I."

Stahl pounded the peddle to the floor. Gray's car rocketed towards the motorcycle. This time, the older woman showed no mercy. She rammed into the cycle's rear tire.

Metal screamed.

Rubber burned.

The cycle swerved for control. If only Stahl showed mercy, it could balance itself. But she had none to offer. The cycle tipped to the side, into the Ford. The driver flew off and slammed into the windshield. The bike pulled under the tires.

The car shook and jolted from treading over the sleek machine, almost snapping the axle and losing speed and a tire.

As the bike filled the rear view mirror, Stahl regained control of the amazingly functional Ford. Miranda stopped screaming and peeked out. The biker was still on the hood, his black-gloved fingers tight in the gap at the windshield and still holding his weapon.

Stahl swerved the car, staying within the lines on the road, and urged the biker off. The man held on despite his legs swinging dangerously close to the edges of the hood.

Once Ruby gave up on that option, the biker, holding on with one hand, aimed at Ruby.

The gun went off.

Ruby jerk the car to the side.

More wild cracks filled the glass but still held together.

The bullet plunged into the car seat above Stahl's shoulder.

Miranda screamed.

Stahl stomped the brake.

The biker flew through the glass, into the car, and darted head-first between the front passenger seats. Stahl lost control of the car, allowing it to run off the asphalt and into a gully dividing it from the trucks and buses-only lane. The sudden dip caused it to flip over, land with its spinning wheels in the air, and skid to stop.

• • • •

"What fucking happened?" Gray screamed from the driver's seat.

Mallory peered out the window with his hands blocking out the interior lights of the ambulance. It helped his view a little but his panting breath fogged up the glass.

"We lost them," he said.

"What do you mean we lost them?" Gray asked.

Prudy knelt on the floor and grabbed Miki's forearm. Her heart pounded and a vice tightened around her brain. She sort of expected this but not really.

"I don't know. I think she ran off the road," Mallory said, leaning away from the window. "But she got one of them. I know that. She ran the fucker over."

"Is she all right?" Gray asked. "What about Church Girl?"

"Dude, I have telekensis. Not ESP."

"Oh, man," Gray said, pounding the wheel. "We have to go back."

Prudy shook her head and pounded her fist on the bench.

"No," Mallory said. "We have to keep going. That was the plan."

"But they need our help," Gray shouted, struggling to keep his eyes on the road. "They could be hurt. Or... Fuck! They could be dead, man."

Prudy shook her head.

"No," Mallory said. "Ruby told us to keep going if anything happened. We have to get Miki to the Colony."

Prudy brought Miki's hand up and kissed it. She groaned, promising to protect her, that she would be okay.

"Are you all right?" Mallory asked. "I mean...shit. I don't know what I fucking mean."

Prudy glanced at him and nodded.

"I know it's hard to do but don't worry," Mallory said. "Don't go crazy. We're still okay. I still got this."

Prudy help up her thumb. Mallory smiled.

A gunshot from outside.

The rear corner of the ambulance tipped. Rubber flopped and metal screeched.

Before Mallory could ask what the hell happened, Gray shouted:

"They shot out our tire!"

• • • •

Despite the pain in her head and the blood dripping from the wound, Stahl found the button to release her seat belt. She dropped to the ceiling of the overturned car and landed on the unconscious, or dead she hoped, biker's legs. Fighting the nausea, she crawled out her open window and stumbled to the other side for Miranda.

"Holy shit," the driver from the parked black SUV said from the shoulder of the Turnpike shouted. A young woman in a tight evening gown to match the young man's tuxedo stood at his side. Amazement covered their sobering faces. "Are you okay?"

Stahl rolled her eyes and pulled open the passenger side door.

"I'm calling an ambulance," the man shouted, pulling his cell phone out.

"Miranda, honey," Stahl said, kneeling to the hanging woman and tapping her bloody face. "Wake up. I know you're alive."

She groaned. Her eyes fluttered.

"Are we there?" she asked.

Stahl smiled and reached for the seat belt buckle.

"Not yet, honey," Stahl said. "We're making a pit stop."

Miranda's eyes widened, realizing where she was and how she got there.

"Oh, Lord! I'm upside down."

"Calm down," Stahl said. "We're okay. But I don't think Gray's car is too good."

"We had an accident," Miranda said. "Why didn't the airbags go off?"

"Honey, you're not thinking straight. I told you. We're in Gray's car."

"Oh," she said. "That's right."

"I'm going to unbuckle you and you're going to drop. I'll help you the best I can" Stahl said. "You ready?"

"I think so."

Stahl counted down from three and clicked the release button. Miranda, with the Stahl supporting her, dropped to the ceiling.

"What happened to that guy?" Miranda asked, shifting her top half to crawl out of the car with Stahl's help.

"He's in there with you."

Miranda glanced behind her and saw the body. With a fresh burst of energy, she quickly crawled out and onto her feet without assistance.

"It's okay," Stahl said, keeping close to her. "He's out cold."

"Is he dead?"

"I don't know," Stahl panted, suddenly feeling weak and dizzy. "I hope so."

"The ambulance and cops are on the way," the tuxedoed driver cheered at the top of the gully. The woman next to him clapped for him, so proud.

Stahl gave him the thumbs up.

"C'mon," she said. "We should move away from the car in case it explodes."

The two women moved around to the other side of the car and started up the gully. Miranda helped Stahl and offered her shoulder for support.

"Do you think the others are okay?" Miranda asked.

"I don't know," Stahl said. "I hope so."

"Look out!" the driver shouted.

The woman with him screamed.

Stahl turned around as a bullet grazed her temple. Another shot went out as Miranda turned around. This one struck her shoulder, inches from her heart. Both women fell and rolled back down the gully to the car.

The biker, panting and holding the smoking gun, Stahl's gun, stood by the front of the Ford. With his free arm, he pulled the helmet off and revealed his angular, sweaty and bloody face.

Stahl blinked and wished she could shake and clear her head but that would only instigate the pain the bullet left in its path. She recognized the biker. It had been years but she definitely recognized him.

"Damien?" she asked.

With pain in his legs, Damien Habsicus shuffled closer to Stahl.

"This is just perfect," he rasped through heavy breath. "I'll be able to scratch you off my shit list."

Stahl gripped his gun with her mind. It was a weak hold due to the pain and disorientation in her brain but strong enough to yank it out of his hand. The gun traveled into the air and landed on the ground behind them.

"Wasn't going to shoot you, Ruby," he said, moving closer. "Strangling you is my pleasure."

When Frank Welker was alive, Stahl learned that Damien had the same ability as Miki Radicci. An empath that experienced others' death and pain. So he's going to enjoy experiencing Ruby's death, his death by his own hands?

"You're sick, Damien," Stahl said.

"I don't care, Ruby."

"Stay away from her," Miranda said, rising to her feet. She held the bullet wound in her shoulder, her arm dangled. "Don't you touch her."

Damien smirked and picked up his helmet. Before Miranda could step around to shield Stahl, he came up to her and cracked the helmet to the side of her skull. Miranda spun around, did a little dance, and fell by the rear of the car.

"There goes your savior," he said, turning his attention back to Stahl. "You really need to recruit more PKs, Ruby. These ESPs are pathetic. Actually, the PKs you recruit are as bad."

"Fuck you," Stahl said, trying to stay conscious, trying to find a little bit of mental focus to defend herself.

"No," he said, standing over her, his legs bent and the helmet in the air to bring down on her face. "Fuck you."

A gun went off and a bullet shot out of Damien's shoulder. He dropped the helmet, spun from the force, and landed on the side of the car.

Miranda, on her knees, shook and aimed Stahl's gun at him.

"I told you to stay away from her," she panted.

Damien laughed and balanced onto his fragile legs. Sirens grew in the air. He glanced at the frightened couple hiding beside their SUV.

"Shit," he rasped. "Don't matter. She's probably dead by now anyway."

Damien shuffled to the front of the car and away from it. He crossed the buses and trucks-only lane and onto the long stretch of untamed land. In the distance, factories and corporate headquarters. With luck, he won't make it far, Stahl hoped.

Miranda dropped to her knees next to Stahl.

"Are you okay?" she asked.

Stahl laughed. The question seemed so absurd. Miranda frowned at the older woman.

"Ruby?" Miranda asked.

Stahl only kept laughing, sparking the pain in her body and keeping her mind alert. She even laughed when the EMTs found their way down to help them.

• • • •

Prudy shook side to side as Gray fought for control of the ambulance. Mallory held the bench. Unsecured medical items fell off the shelf and rained down on them and Miki.

Another gunshot.

The other corner of the ambulance dropped.

"Fuck," Gray shouted. "I have to stop."

Prudy shook her head.

"Don't stop," Mallory said.

A gunshot. One of the front tires popped.

"Shit," Gray said. "They're on my side."

Prudy squeezed her sister's arm tighter and focused on Gray's frightened voice.

A third gunshot was followed by smashed glass.

Gray screamed in pain.

Prudy turned to the window but he wasn't there.

"Gray?" Mallory asked, moving around Prudy and her sister to get to the window. "What happened, man?"

No answer.

The ambulance slowed down.

"Gray, man. Say something," Mallory said, peering through the small open window.

"My fucking shoulder," Gray gasped.

Another bullet plunged through the driver's side window, keeping Gray pressed to the front seat and scaring Mallory away.

The ambulance shook as the bald tires trembled off the smooth asphalt and onto the contoured ground. Mallory stretched his arms on either side of it, standing over the sisters. A moment later, it stopped.

So did the motorcycle engine.

"It's okay," Mallory whispered, sweat drenching his head and shirt. "We're going to be okay. The door is locked and she can't get in."

Metal squeezed and tore. By invisible hands, the back doors ripped off and flew to the sides, landing on the ground. Mallory positioned so all of his size blocked Miki and Prudy. The biker stood outside. Her helmet was gone and her sweaty face was clear. Mallory flinched. It was that crazy chick from back in the winter. The sniper in the woods. Dahlia something. The one who worked with Damien Habiscus to kill Miki and the other psychics.

"Didn't I fuck you up last time?" Mallory asked, smirking.

The blond woman stepped closer. She was unarmed but that didn't matter. She was a PK like him. Mallory walked closer to the edge, hoping to meet her, hoping to jump her, but an invisible vice tightened around his torso. His body lifted and slammed to the roof of the ambulance.

Prudy, stunned, watched her protector try to come down but the Dahlia's invisible hold was too strong. She grabbed a packaged syringe from the mess on the floor and held it like a knife. Prudy rose to attack the woman outside.

"No, don't," Mallory gasped, trying to reach out for her with his pinned arms.

While still holding him to the ceiling, Dahlia shoved Prudy away. The teen dropped on her ass, the needle to the floor, and shook her dazed head when the pressure left her body.

"You fucking psycho bitch," Mallory spat. "She's just a kid."

All her attention on the large black man pinned to the ambulance ceiling, Dahlia released her hold. Mallory slammed to the floor, on his face. A new hold pulled him out of the ambulance. He landed on the ground and slide across the dirt, rocks, and litter far from them.

Dahlia climbed into the back of the ambulance. Prudy, on her knees and facing her, blocked her sister. She pulled the anger into her face and held her hand up as if stopping traffic. The blond chuckled.

The little window into the driver's seat opened and Gray aimed his automatic handgun at the biker.

"Gonno bust your ass, bitch," she shouted.

The blond biker threw a force into the window, making it explode. Screaming, Gray fell back and took a face full of plexiglass with him.

A pressure pushed at Prudy, shoving her to the side and to the wall above the bench. Even though the woman's attention was on Miki, Prudy was pinned and helpless. She watched the skin around Miki's neck push in as if hands or a rope were tightening around it. The life monitor's beeping increased, warning of death.

Prudy struggled against the invisible pressure. She kicked and pushed at the wall. She only exhausted herself and pushed her brain closer to a meltdown. This couldn't be happening. They promised Miki would be fine. They promised to protect her!

Dahlia jolted as if someone behind her shoved her shoulder. Mike Mallory barely stood outside the entrance of the ambulance.

Prudy fell to the bench and scrambled to her sister. Her neck appeared normal. The machine's beeping slowed down.

Facing Mallory, Dahlia gripped Mallory's head with her mind and squeezed it. The large man screamed and grabbed his skull. Pressure built behind his eyes. The world disappeared. But not completely. He focused on her head, too.

Dahlia stumbled back and strengthened her grip on Mallory's skull. Mike, panting, bending forward, squeezed harder around her skull. They both screamed through their pain. Blood leaked from their ears and nose. They were both close to death.

Dahlia was closer.

A staccato of breaking bones. Her skull shattered inward. Blood and brains exploded out through the rips in the flesh. Prudy raised her hands to block the spatter. Blood painted her and Miki. Dahlia dropped dead to the floor. Her head was shaped like a broken hourglass. Mallory feinted.

Gray, his face bleeding and holding his weapon, came around from the front and checked the large man on the ground.

"You okay?" he asked.

Mallory waved him off.

"The girls," he said. "Are they okay?"

"Hold tight, brother," Gray said.

He climbed into the ambulance and accessed the mess. "What the fuck did that fucker do?" He failed to avoid the blood, brains, and body of the biker as he moved closer to Miki and Prudy. "You girls okay?"

Prudy wiped the blood from her eyes and nodded. She grabbed a white towel from the floor and cleaned Miki's face.

"That should be it," Gray said, kneeling beside Prudy, his gun still in his hand and pointing toward Miki. "Just those two, right?"

Prudy nodded and finished clearing Miki's eyes.

They opened and stared at the gun in Gray's hand.

Prudy groaned in joy and grabbed Miki's head to kiss it even though it was matted with blood and brains.

"Why are you pointing a gun at me?" Miki rasped.

"Oh, shit," Gray said. "Smiling." He placed the gun on the floor and glanced outside. Mallory sat up and held his aching head. A drop of blood leaked from his swollen eyes.

"She's awake!" Gray shouted.

"Who's awake?" he asked, suddenly alert.

"Miki's awake, fool," he said, laughing.

Prudy, ever bursting, jumped out of the ambulance and hugged him, her arms barely able to meet at his back. The teen released joyful squeals and grunts. Mallory nearly exploded from the tingles of pride consuming his body.

An explosion Mallory wouldn't have minded.

Tenebrous Chronicles

A majority of my writing focuses on the *Tenebrous Chronicles*. Currently, it encompasses the *Miki Radicci*, the *Radicci Sisters*, and *Cities* series, plus short stories. This is a complete list of the stories in chronological order.

1. Cities That Eat Islands (books 1-3) 1921-1966
2. Fish Hunt (short story) 1921
3. Cities That Hide Bodies (novel) 1967
4. Party Girl Crashes The Rapture (novel) Tenebrous Two
5. Angel Spits (novel) Tenebrous Two
6. A Black Deeper Than Death (novel)
7. The Space Between (short story) Ultimate Omnibus
8. In A Blackened Sky Where Dreams Collide (novel)
9. Bad Land of the Brain (short story) Ultimate Omnibus
10. Blood Like Cherry Ice (novel)
11. The Soul and the Screen (short story) Ultimate Omnibus
12. The Subject (short story)
13. Surely Girly (novel)
14. Genetic Kiss (short story) Ultimate Omnibus
15. Nobody, Nothing (short story) Ultimate Omnibus
16. Bawling Sugar Soul (novel)
17. A Girl and a Gun (short story) Ultimate Omnibus
18. Scorched Heart (short story) Ultimate Omnibus
19. Dick in a Dish (short story) Ultimate Omnibus
20. A Girl Close To Death (novel)

21. Heart on the Devil's Sleeve (novel)
22. Deeper than a Sleepy Head (short story)
23. Sinking Stones in the Sky (novel)
24. Ghost in the Stream (novel)
25. The Lightning From The Fire (short story)
26. Expressway Thru the Skull (novel)
27. Hacker's Moon (novel)
28. Tweens With Pop Guns (short story)
29. Psychic Sisters (novel)
30. Bumper (short story)
31. My Dead Body (novel)
32. Favors (short story)
33. Saints (novel)
34. Squeezed (novel)
35. Broken Psychic Hearts (novel)
36. The Emptiness Above (novel)
37. Rats in a Cage (short story)
38. The Sludge Below (novel)
39. Darby and Cain (short story)
40. The Doe
41. Auties
42. The Killer
43. The Deceiver
44. The Sentinels
45. Six Feet (short story)

BECOME A PATRON NOW BECAUSE THE WORLD NEEDS MORE NEURODIVERGENT CHARACTERS IN ADDICTIVE, THRILLING, AND MYSTERIOUS FICTION!

Patrons are people who financially support my work in exchange for short stories, novels, community, merchandise, and access to special content not found in stores. This support can be as simple as $3 a month to $20.

Check it out at: http://www.patreon.com/mepurfield

About the Author

M.E. Purfield is the autistic author who writes novels and short stories in the genres of crime, sci-fi, dark fantasy, and Young Adult. Sometimes all in the same story. Notably, he works on the Tenebrous Chronicles which encompasses the *Miki Radicci Series*, *The Cities Series*, and the *Radicci Sisters Series*, and also the sci-fi, neuro-diverse *Auts* series of short stories.

Read more at www.patreon.com/mepurfield.